MGNREGA and Women Empowerment

MGNREGA and Women Empowerment

Annita Ranjan

Ocean Books Pvt. Ltd.

ISO 9001:2008 Publishers

Published by
Ocean Books (P) Ltd.
4/19 Asaf Ali Road,
New Delhi-110 002 (INDIA)
e-mail: info@oceanbooks.in

ISBN 978-81-8430-378-0
MGNREGA AND
WOMEN EMPOWERMENT
by Annita Ranjan

Edition
First, 2016

Price
₹ 300.00 (Rupees Three Hundred only)

Printed at
R-Tech Offset Printers, Delhi

For All
whose dreams and struggles
have found a voice in this book!

Voices that seem quiet but
committed to reach beyond!

Melodies produced not by instruments but
through toiling hands with passionate hearts!

Author's Note

A lot has changed in Indian social and economic planning since the introduction of the grand rural employment guarantee scheme, now known as the Mahatma Gandhi National Rural Employment Act, a decade ago. The act has been implemented, suffered setbacks, established landmarks, drawn criticism, and collected accolades in all these years. But most significantly it has profoundly changed the character of the Indian village for good. Whether these changes are good for Indian democracy is a matter of debate, the sides in which are determined by the position on democracy and development taken by the participant. Each side claims support from some observation about the programme. But the people realities are directly affected by the programme have their own perspective.

In writing this book, I have been driven by a desire to bring together the perspectives of the academic specialist, the implementers of the programme, the critics and the advocates, the idealists and the shrewd planners at one place. But above all it is to the lives of the affected people, the poor marginalised beneficiaries of the programme, especially the women that I return for my resources of understanding.

India has leapfrogged towards the direction of being included amongst the rich and powerful countries of the world, and this achievement has been quite impressive; however, there remain concerns, especially the ones that pertain to social welfare of the marginalized communities. It was a positive step on part of the government, in addition to several other steps taken for their welfare, to enact and implement the MGNREGA. The Act was rightly named after Mahatma Gandhi, the Father of the Nation, who dreamed of an India constituting equal people, and where even the last man enjoyed all feasible amenities. The Act has been successful in its purpose to a great extent, though some areas have been a cause of concern, and steps need to be taken to overcome them. It would be pertinent to note that several adequate steps have been taken to strengthen the scheme, and it has displayed appreciable outcomes, with its wide impact on the way of living in rural India. In this book, we seek to present different aspects of the Act, scheme and its implementation so as to give the readers a common insight how successful this scheme has been and what needs to be done. Though the book is based on researches, we have sought to make the reading easy and comprehensible for a common man, so we have declined to mention the studies, as it would have made the reading cumbersome as well as too literal and pedagogic.

I hope that the book would be useful for those who are interested in an informed and passionate debate about social policy in India and in the constitutional vision of bringing dignity to all her citizens.

Ranchi

—Annita Ranjan

Acknowledgements

This small book has taken a long time in the making, and it would have been longer still without the great support from the many friends, I made during my research in the villages in what would still be called the obscure jungles of Jharkhand in academic circles. I am grateful to Manoj for taking me the places that form the core of my research observations, to Rakesh for the incredible help in locating a variety of social classes in the apparently homogeneous rural population of Hazaribagh, and to some of the village representatives for helping me interact with the people in their dialects. Without their support the work would have been a mechanical academic exercise. I want to thank them for turning this into an actual human endeavour.

I am grateful, then, to my academic advisors Late Professor (Dr.) Abdul Khalique for motivating me to think critically about some of the issues that were blurred by political and sociological noise. A special thanks to Prof Zeba, more of a friend than a teacher, for never losing faith in my ability to express bold optimism that informs these pages.

My thanks are due to a host of technical supports that I received from Abhay, Chandra Shekhar and more importantly Achyut Chetan. My better half and more of a friend Manish Ranjan who meticulously read the first draft of the book and did not bat an eyelid when my positions squarely differed from his trained bureaucratic eyes. It has been a long journey, but in his company a fully rewarding one.

And finally I must express my deep gratitude to my lovely mother, sisters Kumkum, Anu, Neetu and caring brothers Jai Prakash and Gyan Prakash for their continued encouragement and blessings which was an inspiring force in completing this book.

Abbreviations Used in the Book

APL	Above Poverty Line
APO	Assistant Programme Officer
ATM	Automated Teller Machine
BC	Business Correspondent
BDO	Block Development Officer
BPL	Below Poverty Line
CAG	Comptroller and Auditor General
CBS	Core Banking System
CDS	Community Development Societies
CERD	Centre for Education and Research Development
CFT	Cluster Facilitation Team
CGP	Cluster of Gram Panchayats
CSO	Civil Society Organisation
e-FMS	Electronic Fund Management System
EGS	Employment Guarantee Scheme
FY	Financial Year
GoI	Government of India
GP	Gram Panchayat
GPRS	General Packet Radio Service
GRS	Gram Rozgar Sevak

GS	Gram Sabha
Ha	Hectares
IAP	Integrated Action Plan
IAY	Indira Awas Yojna
JC	Job Card
MGNREGA	Mahatma Gandhi National Rural Employment Guarantee Act
MIS	Management Information System
MPR	Monthly Progress Report
MR	Muster Roll
NSSO/NSS	National Sample Survey Organization
OBC	Other Backward Classes
Oya	Over a year ago
PDS	Public Distribution System
PIA	Project Implementing Agency
PO	Programme Officer
PRI	Panchayati Raj Institution
RBI	Reserve Bank of India
RTI	Right to Information
SAU	Social Audit Unit
SBI	State Bank of India
SC	Scheduled Caste
SMF	Small and Marginal Farmer
SoRs	Schedule of Rates
ST	Scheduled Tribe

Contents

Introduction

The Preamble of the Indian Constitution declares the lofty ideals of the Indian state as ensuring the dignity of the individual and providing them with 'JUSTICE, social, economic and political' and 'EQUALITY of status and of opportunity' to all its citizens. The Directive Principles of the State Policy clearly articulates the ethical demands that must be put on the state in Article 39 in the following words:

The State shall direct its policy towards securing: adequate means of livelihood to all citizens, a proper distribution of the material resources of the community for the common good, the prevention of concentration of wealth to the common detriment, equal pay for equal work for both men and women, the protection of the strength and health of workers and avoiding circumstances which force citizens to enter avocations unsuited to their age or strength, protection of childhood and youth against exploitation of moral and material abandonment.[1]

Clearly the founders of the Republic were driven by a comprehensive ideal for the whole nation, including its heart settled in its villages. Committed as the State is on behalf of 'We, the people' to protect all its citizens from 'moral and material abandonment' it took a huge step, falteringly and but steadily, towards the planning and implementation of one of the largest programs of social empowerment, the Mahatma Gandhi National Rural Employment Guarantee Act. The Mahatma

Gandhi National Rural Employment Guarantee Act (MGNREGA), 2005, was notified on 7 September 2005 with the avowed objective of providing 100 days of guaranteed wage employment in a financial year to every rural household, whose adult members volunteer to do unskilled manual work.

The MGNREGA, as the acronym goes, and the resultant scheme, aim primarily at ensuring livelihood security to the rural households through guaranteed wage employment. Unlike the previous programmes of employment generation and poverty alleviation, it is aimed at alleviating/mitigating rural poverty. Its other aims include inclusive growth, transparency, decentralized development and participation of civil society in rural and national development. Its other important objectives are to empower the most deprived sections of the society, including women, without intermediaries and to create demand-based local level community assets so as to fill in critical infrastructure gap in the rural area. All these objectives have helped to make the MGNREGA a national project. It is keeping in with the ideology of Mahatma Gandhi, who urged us, in our moments of doubt, to recall the face of the poorest person we may have seen and ask ourselves whether the step we are contemplating is likely to be of any use to him or her. It was in this spirit that the Mahatma Gandhi National Rural Employment Guarantee Act (MGNREGA) was launched in February 2006. It is perhaps the largest and most ambitious social security and public works programme in the world.

In principle, at least, the Act seems to embody the cardinal principle of justice envisaged by some of the greatest social thinkers of the modern world. By bringing the most vulnerable mass of the Indian society at the centre of its action the MGNREGA also seems to be responding to the ethical task set by the great political philosopher John Rawls. In his first statement of the now-classic principles of justice the Rawls' principles read thus:

First: each person is to have an equal right to the most extensive scheme of equal basic liberties compatible with a similar scheme of liberties for others.

Second: social and economic inequalities are to be arranged so that they are both (a) reasonably expected to be to everyone's advantage, and (b) attached to positions and offices open to all.[2]

The principles of justice read well with the vision of our constitutional framework but after several decades of becoming a republic we were yet to make the second principle work to 'everyone's advantage.' We seem to have forgotten that the least advantaged in a democracy are the ones most in need of democratic support. Rawls' famous version of his own second principle of justice, known more famously as the difference principle may be read as one of the driving forces behind the MREGA. It suggests that social and economic inequalities are to be arranged so that they are both (a) to the greatest expected benefit of the least advantaged and (b) attached to offices and positions open to all under conditions of fair equality of opportunity.[3]

The MGNREGA needs to be evaluated as a grand programme of action designed to secure, in Rawlsian terminology, the 'greatest expected benefit of the least advantaged.' Since the objective of this book is also to provide a correct perspective on the future of the programme we will focus on the aspects of the expectations that we can have of it. There have been numerous expressions of skepticism about practicality and viability of this initiative in public and academic discourse, yet in its decade long existence as a practice, the basic soundness and high potential of the MGNREGA are well established.

The following remarkable facts about the programme may help us balance some of the doubts that inform the public perception about its feasibility and the extent of its reach:

(a) Since its inception in 2006, an amount of around Rs. 1,10,000 crore has gone directly as wage payment to rural households and 1200 crore person-days of employment has been generated. On an average, 5 crore households have been provided employment every year since 2008.

(b) Eighty per cent of households are being paid directly through bank/post office accounts, and 10 crore new bank/post office accounts have been opened.

(c) The average wage per person-day has gone up by 81 per cent since the scheme's inception, with state-level variations. The notified wage today varies from a minimum of ₹ 122 in Bihar, Jharkhand to ₹ 191 in Haryana.

(d) Scheduled Castes (SCs) and Scheduled Tribes (STs) have accounted for 51 per cent of the total person-days generated and women for 47 per cent, well above the mandatory 33 per cent as required by the Act.

(e) 146 lakh works have been taken up since the beginning of the programme, of which about 60 per cent have been completed. These include projects relating to rural connectivity (e.g. village roads), water conservation and water harvesting, irrigation canals and renovation of traditional water bodies, flood protection and drought proofing, land development, and work done on private lands (lands belonging to small and marginal farmers/SCs/STs/Below Poverty Line (BPL) households/Indira Awas Yojana (IAY) and land reform beneficiaries).

(f) 12 crore job cards have been given and these along with the 9 crore muster rolls have been uploaded on the Management Information System (MIS), available for public scrutiny. Since 2010–11, all details with regard to the expenditure of the MGNREGA are available on the MIS in the public domain.

Now compare the specific objectives of the programme:

(a) To ensure social protection for the most vulnerable people living in rural India through providing employment opportunities.

(b) To ensure livelihood security for the poor through creation of durable assets, improved water security, soil conservation and higher land productivity.

(c) To strengthen drought-proofing and flood management in rural India.

(d) To aid in empowerment of the marginalized communities, especially women, Scheduled Castes (SCs) and Scheduled Tribes (STs), through the processes of a rights-based legislation.

(e) To strengthen decentralized, participatory planning through convergence of various anti-poverty and livelihoods initiatives.

(f) To deepen democracy at the grass-roots by strengthening the Panchayati Raj Institutions (PRIs).

(g) To effect greater transparency and accountability in governance.

It will be clear from the above comparison and the theoretical contextualization of its larger vision that the MGNREGA has indeed become a powerful instrument for inclusive growth in rural India through its impact on social protection, livelihood security and democratic governance. Over the years, the program has been working to change the basic distributive structure of the

Indian society with a clear focus on the disadvantaged and marginalised poor. Its effects on their lives have been profound and pervasive, and favoured the ones who have long been falling in the shadow of the main beam of the light of development. It directly affects is the vast mass that has no formal moorings and support mechanisms in the fast changing world of economic globalization.

It satisfies some of the crucial principles enshrined in our Constitution and has worked towards a comprehensive removal of inequality from many layers of Indian society. The long term benefits of the Act will be seen not merely in the socio-economic sphere but also in the mitigation of the huge political disasters that the republic has witnessed in its six decades long history.

Coverage: The Act was initially notified in 200 rural districts in its first phase. In FY 2007–08, it was extended to an additional 130 rural districts. The remaining districts were notified under the MGNREGA with effect from 1 April, 2008. Since then, the MGNREGA has covered the entire country with the exception of districts that have a hundred per cent urban population.

Salient Features of the Act

The Act is rich with the following features that make it an effective tool of poverty alleviation in rural India:

(a) **Registration:** Under the Act, each household is entitled to a 100 days of employment every year. Adult members of a rural household, willing to do unskilled manual work, may apply for registration to the local gram panchayat.

(b) **Job Cards:** Only adult members are eligible for employment. A registered household is issued with a job card. It forms the basis of identification for demanding employment. It has to be issued within 15 days of registration. Each job card has a unique identification number and is used to record work and payment made thereof.

(c) **Application for Work:** A written application seeking work has to be made to the gram panchayat or block office, stating the time and duration for which work is sought. The gram panchayat will issue a dated receipt of the written application for employment, against which the guarantee of providing employment within 15 days operates. This application can also be made orally to the concerned official.

(d) **Unemployment allowance:** In case employment is not provided within 15 days, the state will pay an unemployment allowance to the beneficiary.

(e) **Provision of Work:** Work is provided within 5 kilometres radius of the village. In case, it is provided beyond 5 km, extra wages of 10 per cent are payable to meet additional transportation and living expenses. Priority is given to women, such that at least one-third of the beneficiaries under the scheme are women. At least 50 per cent of works, in terms of cost, are to be executed by the gram panchayat.

(f) **Wages:** Wages are to be paid as per the state-wise Government of India notified MGNREGA wages. Wages are also to be paid according to piece rate, as per the Schedule of Rates (SoRs). Payment of wages has to be done on a weekly basis and not beyond a fortnight in any case. Payment of wages is mandatorily done through the individual/joint bank/post office beneficiary accounts.

(g) **Planning:** Plans and decisions regarding the nature and choice of works are to be made in open assemblies of the gram sabha and ratified by the gram panchayat. Works that are inserted at block and district levels have to be approved by the gram sabha before administrative approval can be given.

(h) **Cost Sharing:** The Government of India bears the 100 per cent wage cost of unskilled manual labour and 75 per cent of the material cost, including the wages of skilled and semi-skilled workers.

(i) **Worksite Management:** To ensure that the workers are directly benefitted under the Scheme, the Act prohibits the use of contractors or machinery in execution of the works. To ensure that the spirit of the Act is not diluted and wage employment is the main focus, the MGNREGA mandates that in the total cost of works undertaken in a gram panchayat, the wage expenditure to material expenditure ratio should be 60:40. Worksite facilities such as crŁche, drinking water and shade have to be provided at all worksites.

(j) **Transparency and Accountability:** Transparency and accountability in the programme are ensured through social audit and grievance-redressal mechanisms. Rules have to be put in place for ensuring a responsive implementation process. All accounts and records relating to the scheme should be available for public scrutiny.

This book addresses MGNREGA from with an aggregating attitude, analysing its value not just in one aspect but in the entire range of its execution. The elusive but indispensable goal of equal citizenship and equal distribution of primary goods is the standard against which the program is evaluated in the book. This is evident from the vast scope of the program that leaves no aspect of the rural Indian political economy untouched. To be fair, the program indirectly affects the entire macroeconomic infra-system of the nation, and paves way for a gradual change in our society.

An Unprecedented Scope

The MGNREGA is unprecedented in several aspects. It is unlike any other programme so far its scale, construction and thrust are concerned. It has an integrated natural resource management and livelihoods generation perspective. Its transparency and accountability mechanisms create unprecedented accountability of performance, especially towards immediate stakeholders. Some of its other major aspects are outlined below:

(a) Unlike the earlier wage employment programmes that were allocation-based, the MGNREGA is demand-driven and the transfer of resources from Government of India to states is based on the demand for employment in each of the states. This provides an additional incentive for the states to leverage the Act to meet the employment needs of the poor.

(b) It provides a legal guarantee of wage employment.

(c) It is a demand-driven programme where provision of work is triggered by the demand for work by wage-seekers.

(d) Its design is people-centred, demand-driven, self-selecting and rights-based.

(e) It has legal provisions for allowances and compensation, in case of failure to provide work on demand, and delays in payment of work undertaken. In case work is not provided on time, the states bear the cost of unemployment allowance.

(f) It overcomes problems of targeting through its self-targeting mechanism of beneficiary selection.

(g) It gives incentives to states to provide employment as 100 per cent of the unskilled labour cost and 75 per cent of the material cost of the programme is borne by the Government of India.

(h) The order of devolution of financial resources to gram panchayats is unprecedented as they are authorized to implement 50 per cent of the works in terms of cost.

(i) A Report on the outcomes of MGNREGA is presented annually by the Government of India to the Indian Parliament and by the state governments to the state legislatures.

(j) Social audit, a new feature of the MGNREGA, creates unprecedented accountability of performance, especially towards the immediate stakeholders.

In view of the above features, the MGNREGA is a massive and effective step on part of the Government of India to create employment as well as boost development in rural India. It has definite repercussions on several aspects of personal, social, development and national domains, so there is need to study it in a greater detail. The book studies the program as an excellent example of the benefits and of state activism which addresses the interests of its disadvantaged citizens and attempts to balance its own acts of liberalization and privatization that seem to have become geopolitical compulsion in these days of globalization. The next chapters of the book hope to examine both, the conditions in which MGNREGA operates and the conditions that it helps to transform and recreate.

1

Empowering the Marginalised

Mahatma Gandhi is supposed to have identified complete freedom with the wiping off of the last tear from the last distressed eyes in India. That would be the achievement of true democracy in India. As Amartya Sen and Jean Dreze have argued, a just democratic politics in India must recognize 'the necessity of paying much greater attention to the interests, demands and rights of the most deprived (as opposed to the relatively disadvantaged among the more advantaged).'[4] The MGNREGA, apart from actively implementing the social vision of the Indian Constitution also acknowledges the shrewd economic insight that the well-being of the people, particularly the less advantaged is of greatest urgency for the functioning of Indian economy.[5]

The chief objective of the MGNREGA is to provide a steady source of income and livelihood security for the poor, the vulnerable and the marginalized. It has a great impact on poverty and inclusive growth. Overall evidence suggests that it does provide basic income assurance to a large number of beneficiaries. In Financial Year 2011–12 alone, nearly 5 crore households (close to 25 per cent of all rural households in the country) were provided over 209 crore person-days of work. The MGNREGA has provided around ₹ 1, 10,700 crore (66 per cent of the total expenditure of around ₹ 1,66,000 crore) as worker wages from FY 2006 to FY 2011–12. It has a positive impact on household income, monthly per capita expenditure, food security and health of the beneficiaries, with greater potential in terms of poverty alleviation at a high scale, that can be realized.

As an observer had noted with a critical hope during the inception of the programme, the rural employment guarantee scheme was considered as absolutely essential for India for poverty reduction, prevention of starvation, reducing distressed migration of the poor and empowerment of the poor. This act also has the potential to direct strategic use of surplus labour for promoting sustainable development and for mainstreaming the poor in the economy.[6]

Evidently the program was aimed at reducing poverty but with a clear long term vision of mainstreaming the poor in the economy. Thus, we use the term marginal in the double sense of disenfranchised poor and also the section of people excluded from the mainstream of economy. A fair understanding of the program can only be possible when we recognize how far these goals have been achieved.

The following brief overview of its dynamic overall impact in this regard may help us in this task:

1. Household Income: There are a number of ways in which the MGNREGA impacts poverty, the most direct and obvious way being by providing extra work opportunities. There is also preliminary evidence from the field that MGNREGA income is being used by rural households for starting their own ventures.
2. Alternative Employment Options: In order to estimate the MGNREGA's impact on income more accurately, studies suggest that it is

necessary to deduct the opportunity cost of time (cost of the next best alternative foregone) from the MGNREGA earnings. For example, in Rajasthan, among female-headed households, the share of MGNREGA earnings was found to be nearly 15 per cent of household income; this is slightly higher than twice that of male-headed households, implying substantially greater importance of this source of income to female-headed households. It was found that around 67 per cent of the households said they use the MGNREGA as a source of income when no other work was available.

3. Monthly Per Capita Expenditure: The MGNREGA has resulted into increased monthly per capita expenditure which has been used as a proxy indicator to measure the impact of the MGNREGA on poverty levels of a household. The impact is likely to be positive if the increase in income has translated into an increase in expenditure, particularly on food and essential items, of the household. It follows from a study conducted in Andhra Pradesh that the MGNREGA has caused a significant increase in monthly per capita consumption expenditure of around 10 per cent for households. Expenditure on non-food consumables has increased significantly by around 23 per cent. Expenditure on transportation decreased significantly due to the MGNREGA by around 65 per cent. This is most likely because the MGNREGA stipulates that employment be provided within 5 kilometres of the residence. Similar expenditure patterns were apparent in other states too. The wage-seekers were spending their additional wages from the MGNREGA mainly on food, clothing, education and health care.

4. Impact on Food Security, Savings and Health Outcomes: Deprivation of a wide range of nutrients can lead to a poverty trap where low nutrition leads to low productivity, which in turn leads to low wages and then to low nutrition, thus completing a vicious cycle. The MGNREGA has contributed to ensuring a higher intake of food and food availability. A few research studies also observe that the MGNREGA has had an impact on the health of beneficiaries. Research suggests that welfare costs of economic crises and weather shocks are disproportionately large for the poor who lack the means to protect themselves from adverse income and employment shocks. This could further reinforce existing inequalities, create persistent poverty and hurt the pace of poverty reduction. Through its impact on income, consumption, food security and employment, the MGNREGA appears to be helping in protecting the poor and the vulnerable. For instance, according to a secondary analysis of the MGNREGA data from Andhra Pradesh, a study observed that the scheme provides income for poor households when they need it most, i.e. when they are hit by adverse weather conditions and their farming is adversely affected.
5. MGNREGA and Market Wages: The MGNREGA entitles every worker to wages at the Government of India notified, state-wise wage rate for each day of work. Its notified wage rates have increased across states over the years, with some states like Maharashtra registering an increase of over 200 per cent. The MGNREGA wage is higher than the legal minimum agriculture wage in 19 states.

If we read these achievements against the grain of the image of the poor that Indira Hirway had portrayed in the above quoted article we will conclude that the program has been successful to a great degree in some areas whereas some areas need more attention now She had described the poor, the marginalized, the potential beneficiaries of the programme as 'highly vulnerable to various risks.' According to her, their coping strategies tend to make them even more so. Reduced food consumption, mortgage/sale of assets, borrowings at high interest rates, and migration push them further into the poverty trap. One major solution to their poverty is the provision of minimum income to them through productive employment.[7]

The following survey of the participation of the marginalized is based on an understanding of the idea of marginalization that had informed these discursive moments of the conceptualization of the programme.

Participation of the Marginalised Communities

The MGNREGA employment is simply the most sought by the most-needy. In a survey conducted in 2008 in six states: Bihar, Chhattisgarh, Jharkhand, Madhya Pradesh, Rajasthan and Uttar Pradesh; it was found that a majority of the MGNREGA workers belong to the most disadvantaged sections of society; 81 per cent of the sample workers lived in kutcha (non-permanent) houses, 61 per cent were illiterate, and 72 per cent have had no electricity at home. The SC and ST families accounted for 73 per cent of the workers in the randomly selected sample. At the national level, the share of SCs and STs in the work provided under the MGNREGA has been high at 40–50 per cent. In case of both SCs and STs, the participation rate exceeds their total share in the total population with an exception in Maharashtra.

Other field studies corroborate the high workforce participation by the marginalized. A study conducted in five districts of Uttar Pradesh noted that in its sample, around 85 per cent of the beneficiaries belong to Below Poverty Line (BPL), 50 per cent belong to SCs, 45 per cent belong to the Other Backward Classes (OBCs). An NSSO survey observed that in Andhra Pradesh 42 per cent of the beneficiaries were SCs/ STs and 50 per cent were OBCs, these proportions in Madhya Pradesh were 67 per cent and 29 per cent, and in Rajasthan 50 per cent and 42 per cent, respectively.

Works on Private Lands of the Marginalized and Its Advantages

The Act allows works, such as irrigation, horticulture, land development, on private land belonging to the SCs and the STs or BPL families, as well as to other sections of the marginalized people. Twelve per cent of the total works in FY 2011–12 alone were on lands of individual beneficiaries. Permitting private works on lands implies coverage of 40 per cent of all cultivated area (80 per cent of all land holdings). In this way, the MGNREGA can play a significant role in raising the agricultural productivity of these farmers who will then be able to return to farming and will no longer need to depend on the scheme for their survival. This is a step in the direction of moving from unskilled manual labour to skilled farming practices. It is interesting to note that since the inception of the programme (as per MIS/Monthly Progress Reports), out of the total individual beneficiaries (on whose land work has been undertaken) almost 50 per cent have not sought employment under the scheme, following the work on their land. This may suggest that the MGNREGA is realizing its objective in making these farmers self-dependent.

The MGNREGA in Districts Experiencing Left-Wing Extremism

The MGNREGA was also introduced in the

states suffering from Left-wing extremism, such as Chhattisgarh, Jharkhand and Odisha. The following trends are seen in it so far as the affected districts in these states are concerned:

1. Employment and Work Participation: With limited employment opportunities, outside the MGNREGA, all three states have low average annual days of employment; in Odisha average days of employment were 35–40 days, in Chhattisgarh 60–70 days and in Jharkhand 150 days. Thus, the MGNREGA provides additional employment days and is an important source of supplementary income.
2. Wages: Wages in different agriculture operations have gone up following the introduction of the MGNREGA. Pre-MGNREGA wages for women were in the range of ₹ 20/day (in Bastar, Chhattisgarh) to around ₹ 55/day (in Khunti, Jharkhand). Wages for men were in the range of ₹ 37/day (in Gumla, Jharkhand) to ₹ 75/day (in Khunti, Jharkhand). Post-MGNREGA, the wages for men and women have gone up to the range of ₹ 80/day (in Bastar, Chhattisgarh) to ₹ 105/day (in Dhamtari, Chhattisgarh). The study suggests that the increase in female wages was greater than that of men.
3. Household Income: The increase in overall employment and wages has also resulted in an increase in household income. In Chhattisgarh, the increase in household income ranged from 23-160 per cent, in Jharkhand it ranged from 60-70 per cent and in Odisha it ranged from 30-40 per cent over the decade.

Micro-level data also indicates the positive impact of the scheme on the marginalized people. A study in Madhya Pradesh shows that the beneficiaries found the work quality to be very good. On the one hand, the MGNREGA increases the purchasing power of the workers creating demand for commodities. This has been regarded as an important contributor to soften the impact of worldwide recession on the Indian economy. At the same time, by generating incomes for small and marginal farmers, the MGNREGA stimulates private investment on these farms. Effectively a wage employment programme can thus be transformed into a source of sustainable livelihoods generating self-employment. This would permit reductions in allocations for MGNREGA over time, not only because landed labourers get back to their own farms, but also because of a general rise in demand for labour in rural economy.

The crucial point that emerges from the discussions so far, including MGNREGA's impact on areas under the reactionary jurisdiction of left wing extremism is its extremely flexible and accommodating role in giving an economic cushion to a collective despair which is fast disappearing. It is not surprising that the programme has such a significant role to play not merely in establishing a just redistributive procedure but also in conveying an arrival of justice among the marginalized. As noted by Sen and Dreze, the program has made 'impressive changes in the wage relations, particularly of casual labour,' and which in turn has 'significantly multiplied the income-generation effects of the programme'.[8] The programme has significantly been able to contain the inevitable violence that the global restructuring of economy in the post-liberalization economy is causing. A profound aspect of the empowerment of the marginalized through this programme is that it has brought them into the currency of demand, not just for the labour but also for what they produce.

The superficial criticism that all MGNREGA work is equivalent is just 'playing with mud' has been disproved by many surveys including the Dreze and Khera who reported that more than ninety percent of EGA workers consider their work useful or even 'very useful.' According to their survey, eighty-one percent of the field investigators find the work useful and consequential.[9] The validity of such claims were attested to by the economist Prabhat Pattanaik who had initially argued there was an assumption 'that there would be enough unutilised capacity...for the scheme':

Production in any sector requires, as current inputs, materials and labour. The wages given to labour in turn are spent partly on food and partly on non-food consumption goods. The employment projects under this scheme then would be generating current demand for material inputs, for food grains and for non-food (mainly industrial) consumption goods. These sectors, for meeting this additional demand, would need to produce more, and hence would generate, in turn, current demand for their material inputs and for more labour, and hence for more food grains and non-food consumption goods, and so on.[10]

The conception of the MGNREGA and its later implementation, thus, despite several glitches have led to a robust empowerment of the marginalized. They have been empowered not merely in their specific local context of employment but, as shown by the above cited evidence, have been brought into the circuit of mainstream labour and employment. This will have significantly positive effect on the marginalized, including women to whom we turn in our next chapters.

□

2

Engendering Social Empowerment

The MGNREGA is recognized as a tool of gender equity and empowerment. Many commentators have stressed upon the gender dimension of its impact, particularly in north India.[11] This has happened not as a supplementary benefit of the programme as a consequence of the gender-sensitive planning that has informed it at its inception. Various provisions under it aim to ensure that women have equitable and easy access to work, decent working conditions, equal payment of wages and representation on decision-making bodies. For example, the Act makes it compulsory to that one-third of the workers are women. Since the Act does not impose any limitations on how each house holds' quota of 100 days is shared within the household, women's participation in work under the MGNREGA is facilitated at several informal levels. Most importantly, the wage earned is equal for both men and women. In the informal work sector to which the Act primarily caters, this is a revolutionary step towards gender-equality. When there are more than five children under six years of age are present at the worksite the Act provides for on the spot childcare facilities. This is an important provision given that, in large parts of the country, there are no childcare arrangements (e.g., functional Angan wadis) for working women.

According to the NREGA Survey 2008 From Financial Year 2006–07 up to FY 2011–12, around ₹ 53,000 crore have been spent on wages for women and around 47 per cent of the total person-days generated have been by women. While there is not much scope for skepticism about the ideals of gender equality embedded in the programme it would be a mistake to assume that there is a smooth translation of concepts into action in a deeply gendered society like India. Empowerment, either aided by the state or autonomously designed, inevitably happens along an axis of gender in any society. It is important to remember that MGNREGA work, despite the best intentions of its framers or probably because of their deliberate choice allows certain possibilities of dissolving the boundaries between work and house-work, while firmly maintaining that all work done under it fetches equal wages no matter what the sex of the worker is. As a result, MGNREGA also compels a society to redefine work and non-work. In terms of status-production, as defined by Hannah Papanek, the program has far reaching consequence. Papanek argued that although women's work is not always visible and classifiable in terms productivity, it is accepted by 'many women as part of their self-definition.' Status production, she argues, 'refers to the latent meaning of work, and it appears to be a useful analytic construct in the understanding of women's and men's work'.[12] MGNREGA has created a long term impact in making women's work productive of status. This status, in turn, has given a completely new gender shift to the process of empowerment, pushing it beyond the confines of mere economic rise to an overall enhancement of the emotional, psychological and political consciousness of women.

So, it would be prudent to study the impact of this scheme on economic and social empowerment of women.

Women Participation in the MGNREGA

Women are participating in the scheme more actively than in other works as can be gauged from their national participation rate of 47 per cent. Research indicates that it is an important work opportunity for women who would have otherwise remained unemployed or underemployed.

At the national level, participation of women in the scheme has surpassed the statutory minimum requirement of 33 per cent; in FY 2011-12 alone, women person-days of employment was close to 50 per cent. Thus, women's share on works under it is greater than their share of work in the casual wage labour market across all states. Women are participating in the scheme much more actively than they participated in all other forms of recorded work. It brings out the fact that the MGNREGA creates decent and favourable work conditions for women. For instance, it stipulates work to be given within 5 kilometres of the village where the job applicant resides, it makes logistically feasible for the women to participate who otherwise may have limited employment opportunities available to them, given their role and responsibilities in their households. A study conducted in Bihar, Chhattisgarh, Jharkhand, Madhya Pradesh, Rajasthan and Uttar Pradesh seems to confirm these findings. The southern states, like Kerala and Tamil Nadu, show a higher rate of participation in the MGNREGA as compared to their overall work participation in all other recorded works. Among the northern and some eastern states, however, the pattern has been generally different, with proportionately fewer women working in the scheme than in other rural work; Rajasthan is the only exception.

It has also been found that in places where market wages are higher than the MGNREGA, men undertake jobs in the market and women seek employment under the Scheme. Non-availability of worksite facilities like crŁches, is also a huge disincentive for women. Further, certain types of work also limit their participation.

Reduced Differential Wages and Wage Parity

The MGNREGA has reduced traditional wage discrimination in public works. Average wage for labour in MGNREGA was ₹ 90.9 per day for men, and for women it was ₹ 87 per day. The difference was larger for labour in other public works; ₹ 98.3 per day for men and ₹ 86.1 per day for women. Other studies also suggest an upward movement of unskilled wages for women post-MGNREGA. For instance, in Kerala, the wages for women in agriculture and forest work rose from ₹ 70-80 in 2007 to ₹ 110-125 in 2009. In fact, real wages increased more rapidly for female workers than for male workers. Parity in wage rates also appears to be positively affecting participation of women in the scheme. When casual labour market opportunities are better for men than for women, it is easier for the latter to get the (limited) number of jobs available under the scheme, though Punjab (at 43 per cent participation of women) and Haryana (at 36 per cent) appear to be the exceptions.

Economic Independence and Empowerment of Women

It has been seen in preliminary findings that the increased access to paid work due to the MGNREGA has had a positive impact on women's socio-economic status and general well-being. In a survey conducted across six states, 82 per cent of the widows regarded the MGNREGA as a very important source of income, and of the total sample, 69 per cent of the women stated that it helped them avoid hunger. Findings from different studies reveal that post-MGNREGA, women have greater control over their wages and have been spending them on repaying small debts, paying for their children's schooling and bearing medical expenses, and the like.

Improved access to economic resources and paid work has had a positive impact on the socioeconomic status of women. In a survey, it was revealed that it is very advantageous for the poorest of the poor. This was also apparent in the findings of another study which concluded, where migration to urban areas offers relatively higher incomes for men, much of the MGNREGA workers were found to be women and older men who had discontinued migration.

Thus, it has helped women to exercise independence in collecting and spending the MGNREGA wages, indicating greater decision-making power within the households. In Andhra Pradesh, it was found that almost 47 per cent of the respondents received wages themselves, 50 per cent received wages along with their husbands and wages of around 4 per cent of respondents were paid to their husbands; while in Rajasthan, almost 91 per cent of women received wages themselves.

In a large number of cases, women indicated that they had a substantial say in the way this money was spent. They were able to utilize the money for avoiding hunger, repaying small debts, paying for their child's schooling and bearing medical expenses.

The women employed under the MGNREGA have also reported better access to credit and financial institutions. The mandatory transfer of wage payment through bank accounts has ensured that a greater number of women are brought into institutional finance from which they had been largely excluded. Research suggests that qualitative and quantitative improvements in gender equations across various spheres (social, political and economic) coupled with positive changes in self-perception gradually result in the empowerment of women and engender a lasting social change. A study conducted in Meghalaya suggests that the necessity of interacting with the bank/post office/government officials has empowered rural tribal women by enhancing their confidence level and ensuring some degree of independence, both in matters of finance and decision-making. For example, the role of women was limited in the traditional Khasi society, but it is no more so where they have taken up jobs under the MGNREGA.

Reservation for women in the MGNREGA has helped them seek representation in decision-making bodies, including the village employment councils. To address some of these concerns, the scheme has incorporated particular provisions related to gender-specific lifecycle needs, such as allowing time off for breastfeeding and flexibility in terms of women's working hours, so that they can balance their domestic care and work responsibilities.

MGNREGA, Women's Livelihood Security in Conjunction with Ecology

Since the MGNREGA plays an important role in natural resource regeneration, the scheme seems to be strengthening livelihood security for women. It links environment and livelihood security as women rely heavily on natural common property resources like water, fuel etc. A large majority of them are dependent on agriculture. Thus, where household access to water and fuel relies heavily on common property, local resources are clearly a major source of well-being, or risk. Migration leads to extra hardships for women since men tend to migrate leaving the womenfolk behind to look after their property and household. In dry land areas, female-headed households are often the ones which are the poorest, so women have to put in significantly extra efforts.

The MGNREGA, through the creation of sustainable rural assets, water conservation and forestry works, has the potential to contribute to ecological restoration and generate environmental benefits through increased livelihood security, especially for rural women, to climate change and other shocks. The problem they face in household provisioning in areas of high dependence on natural resources is due to a lack of defined rights over community assets. At present a large number of women workers have minimal rights to the productive assets they work on even under the scheme, and this contributes to persistence of social exclusion. Organizational arrangements at the local level are needed to reduce the problem of implementation of gender-specific policy measures. These may include rights to maintenance, sharing etc. Thus, several steps are needed to be taken for their empowerment, though many of their issues have been addressed marginally well.

The Shift in Perspective

The above discussion enables us to discuss the otherwise unquantifiable aspect of the gendering of social empowerment that MGNREGA has slowly caused. The gendering of work and its relationship with social structure is beautifully described by Hannah Papanek in her discussion segregation. She argues that

The nature of occupational segregation by gender ("women's jobs" and "men's jobs") and the extent of women's participation in specific occupations by class should be seen as a concrete expression of that society's value system about the allocation of labor between women and men.[13]

Without much reformist fervour the program achieves this restructuring of the system of allocation. The program however needs to go beyond implementation of the several provisions that address the issue of women's participation. These provisions may not be uniformly successful in all cases and in all states. Some of them face more resistance in implementation than others.

However, it is evident after numerous surveys that participation in MGNREGA work even at a small level can have profound effect on women's visibility and social status. Women's visibility makes them important actors in local planning for development and draw the attention of the regional state authorities to problems that would not have appeared on their mind so far. Problems like the unavailability of crŁches for mothers of young children and the continued illegal presence of contractors get attention and in many reported cases have been sorted out by the local administration much to the satisfaction and security of the women.

MGNREGA has made significant gains in the for women workers—in accessing work and an income, food and healthcare for themselves and their families, and in leaving potentially hazardous work. There are several ways in which the programme has affected gender relations in the rural areas under its field of influence. Ideally, employment can and does enhance women's economic independence. Cash earnings foster a sense of equality with men and has far reaching consequences for gender relations. By changing the gendered segregation of labour, the gendered division of labour, the program has begun to change the social perception of women. They are now understood as active contributors to the local and national economy in their own might.

Provisions of local self-governance under panchayati raj institutions have also been complemented by MGNREGA programmes, and have generated a new form of female political surveillance, a new act of citizenship that makes the state and the society more responsible to the specific needs and desires of its female population. We still hope that these besides these provisions, something like a comprehensive perspective on gender equality will soon be built in by the Act. As Reetika Khera and Nandini Nayak have suggested,

One of the first steps in this direction is to move from the household entitlement of 100 days to individual entitlements, which will assure women 100 days of work in their own right, without having to negotiate within the household.[14]

Such actions, combined with an 'increase in the share of women in staff appointments would also go a long way towards achieving the agenda of gender equality and sensitivity.'[15] Khera and Nayak sum up of the prospects of gender relations and their just improvement in their views in these words:

> For the longer term goals of gender equality to be realised, attention also needs to be paid to ensuring greater participation of women at all levels (e.g., as labourers, in NREGA worksite management and staff appointments) and in all spheres (e.g., participatory planning through participation in gram sabhas, social audits). These measures can simultaneously impact gender relations and improve the implementation of NREGA.

We can certainly hope that the longer the program works in any given area it will inevitably lead to complex sociological changes in the gendered aspects of a society. It will break a few traditional hierarchies, and steadily dismantle age old prejudices about work and its artificially generated gender. Women will be restored to a position of active social agents, with substantial autonomy and self-worth; and it will have long term impact on the questions of health, child-care, ecological balance and also create a healthy balance between the rural economy and the domestic economies of the family.

□

3

Modernity and Women Under the MGNREGA

One of the most vigorous and famous debates during the foundation of the Indian Republic was staged in the Constituent Assembly of India, when BR Ambedkar, the chief architect of the Constitution castigated Indian intellectuals for their 'infinite if not pathetic love' for the village. An intense debated ensued following Ambedkar's characterization of the villages as 'a sink of localism, a den of ignorance, narrow-mindedness and communalism.'[16] Ambedkar saw more clearly than the others the pervasive contradictions between the hierarchical social structures inherited from the past and the urge for a democratic legal and political order forcefully expressed in the Assembly. Like the other members of it, he too had expectations about the future, but unlike most of them he did not have illusions about the past.[17] To him the Constitution was an instrument to bring modernity to rural India.

The village has been central to the debate about modernity in India, and women and gender relations constitute an important core of the contours of modernity in rural India. The MGNREGA is possibly the grandest programme of action that directly seeks to negotiate this complex question about women and modernity in India. In this chapter, I have attempted to understand this vexed issue in all its aspects, social, cultural and economic and examine if the MGNREGA has indeed brought in any transformation in the consciousness of women in rural India. Have they, after all, responded well to the challenge thrown by Dr. Ambedkar at the founding moment of the nation? To answer this question we have taken an extremely close look at all the intricacy of women's lives as affected by the program in the Hazaribagh district of Jharkhand. The data has been collected from 320 rural women of the district through stratified random sampling method.[18] Out of these 320 rural women, 160 belong to those who have worked under the MGNREGA while the other 160 have not. In order to examine the impact of the MGNREGA on overall modernity of rural women, participants of the MGNREGA constitute the experimental group, while the other non-participants form the control group. These two groups have been further analyzed by dividing them into two age groups of 21-30 and 35-45 years. The respondents have also been divided on the basis of the level of their literacy. The study also attempts to further analyze data on the basis of family size.

However, let us first deal with the term 'modernity'. It encapsulates the progress of societies from primitive civilizations which evolved steadily through distinct stages, arriving at a modern age characterized by industrialization and capitalism, culminating in the current, post-modern state of globalization which shapes contemporary society with ever-increasing momentum. A defining feature of modernity is the realization of democracy, demanded by free-thinking people originating from the Industrial Revolution in western Europe throughout the mid-eighteenth century, and the French Revolution of 1789.

This term has come to be widely employed to describe the characteristics in technological, political, economic and social development. It owes its special significance to its dynamic character and its universal impact on human affairs. It stems initially from attitudes, a belief that the society can be transformed. Thus, such scientific miracles as test-tube babies, space satellites, nuclear reactors and less spectacular ones which have become commonplace things of developed societies like air conditioning, long distance telephone calls and open heart surgeries are the common examples of modernity.

Modernity is also employed to indicate the process of westernization, particularly to describe the impact of western countries on eastern countries in the recent times. In addition, it is also used in relation to time. The present is modern and the past is traditional. Anything new is modern and everything old is traditional. Thus, modernity is antonym to tradition. Anything opposed to tradition ipso facto becomes modern. Modernity, therefore, is a much used and abused word, used in a positive as well as negative sense. There is fascination and admiration for it, as well as derision and ridicule. It is indicative of glorious human achievement as well as perverse and debased values and behaviour.

Apart from physical attributes, modernity has a psychological concept relating to specific values and attitudes. It is committed to individual dignity, equality and freedom. It has strong beliefs in secularism and prefers democratic and socialistic forms of socio-political organization, combining individual growth with social responsibility and inculcating values and attitudes related to the individual's thought process. A person having strong values and attitudes will be modern irrespective of his external appearance. Thus, Gandhi with his traditional, even primitive, dress of loin cloth was more modern in thinking than Paris-tailored three-piece suit donners. A Middle East Sheikh, despite his abundant wealth, is less modern than a poor Indian tribal who believes in equality of the sexes. Thus, modernity may be defined as a syndrome of personality and attitudinal traits which encourage humanism and rationalism; help personal growth and well-being; facilitate adjustment to a plural and democratic society; and provide psychological qualities for economic development.

Within the Indian context, innumerable changes have taken place in the social fabric over the years. The country has had a rich cultural history which has been found to be closely associated with the prevailing social dynamics, cultures and traditions. These changes have definitely had a bearing on the country's overall progression and the society has exhibited trends that have inculcated the concepts of modernity within them. However, a closer look presents a contrasting picture, with certain social groups remaining untouched by the process of change and modernity. The Indian society traditionally has been less receptive to women, and there are innumerable instances where women have been subjected to untoward and unnecessary social customs and traditions. However, a reflection of recent years, has presented a changing picture with women adopting and inculcating modern traditions and changes impacting all spheres of their lives. These changes have been more perceptible in the urban areas as compared to rural areas. This can be primarily attributed to relatively more women empowerment in the urban areas. To bolster this trend, the government has undertaken and implemented various schemes over the years to improve the prevailing socio-cultural situation for rural women.

The MGNREGA is considered to be an important milestone in this direction, which primarily aims at improving women's participation in society through the creation of employment opportunities. In this context, the current study has been undertaken to assess the impact of the MGNREGA on overall modernity of rural women. Thus, overall modernity constitutes an important aspect of women's life-style, personality and adjustment, and therefore, needs to be measured and studied scientifically.

As seen in the last chapter, the MGNREGA, as a scheme, promises a lot from the perspective of women's empowerment. The act stipulates that wage will be equal for men and women and is also committed to ensuring that at least 33% of the workers shall be women. It thus bridges the gap between men and women for gainful employment as well as wage rates. Thus, the MGNREGA can play a substantial role in economically empowering women and laying the basis for greater social freedom and self-esteem. Current government data substantiate this fact and present an impressive participation of women in the scheme. It is above 33 percent in 15 states with Tamil Nadu (82%), Kerala (71.39%) and Rajasthan (69%) showing highest participation, while states like Bihar and Jharkhand with 26.62 percent and 27.17 percent are lagging behind.

A critical appraisal of the MGNREGA brings to the fore that women's empowerment was not among the original intentions of the scheme and was neither among its main objectives. However, provisions like priority for women in the ratio of one-third of total workers, equal wages for men and women and crŁches for the children of women workers were made in the Act, with a view of ensuring that rural women would benefit from the scheme in a certain manner. Provisions like work within a radius of five kilometres from the house, absence of supervisor and contractor, and flexibility in terms of choosing period and months of employment were not made exclusively for women, but have, nevertheless, been conducive to rural women.

On the flipside, the nature of manual work and wages based on piece rate make it difficult for women to earn minimum wages. Field reports suggest exclusion of single, divorced and separated, and old women in some places. In addition, entitlement to 100 days of guaranteed employment is applicable at the household level. In a male-dominant patriarchal society, it is difficult to believe that women's decision to avail of employment under the MGNREGA would get precedence over the decision of male family members.

Nevertheless, women have availed of the paid employment opportunity under the MGNREGA in large numbers. Women workers had a national average share of 40.65% of total person-days in 2006-07, 42.52% in 2007-08, and 47.88% in 2008-09, exceeding expectations and the stipulated 33% share. Interestingly, this has occurred largely spontaneously. Women's participation under the MGNREGA, measured in person-days, also exceeded their participation in erstwhile employment generation programmes like the Sampoorna Gramin Rojgar Yojana (SGRY) and the Maharashtra Employment Guarantee Scheme (MEGS) less than 50% in 2007-08. It exceeded the national average (viz., 47.88%) in Andhra Pradesh, Gujarat, Kerala, Tamil Nadu, Karnataka, Rajasthan, and Tripura in all the three years. On the other hand, the share of women in total person-days was less than the national average in Bihar, Chhattisgarh, Haryana, Himachal Pradesh, Jharkhand, Maharashtra, Orissa, Punjab, Uttar Pradesh and Uttarakhand (except in 2007-08), West Bengal, and most of the north-eastern states. Further, there is a gap of about 80 percentage points between the states with the highest (and lowest participation) rates, that is, Kerala (85.01%) and Jammu and Kashmir (5.76%). Even if we consider Jammu and Kashmir as outliers, there is still a gap of about 67 percentage points between Kerala and U.P. (18.11%).

Moreover, there are pronounced regional north-south variations. The four southern states, namely, Andhra Pradesh, Karnataka, Kerala, and Tamil Nadu with relatively better human and gender development indices have ensured high participation of women in all the three years, although average person-days is low in Kerala. Rajasthan, with its high women's participation, is the exception among the north Indian states.

In contrast to the high participation of women in the programme as workers, their participation in processes like work selection, social audit, mobilization of civil society, and share in the control and management of assets created is not encouraging. This being the case, in some places, women's participation in the gram sabha has still increased, and there is even an increase in the number of women speaking in the gram sabha. In Madhya Pradesh, women form part of vigilance committees, and it is reported that women are the most vocal among the members of the vigilance committee in some places. There are also some examples of women's groups playing an important role in the management of community assets, for example, in Jatropha plantations in Chhattisgarh. Nonetheless, the disjunction between work participation and process participation remains, and it reduces the larger potential community-level impacts of the scheme.

There are various explanations for the varying participation of women workers under the MGNREGA. The factors that have encouraged women workers' participation include the nature of job not requiring any special knowledge and skill; outmigration of male family members; employment opportunity being available at the doorstep; a tradition of rural women working in others' fields; provision of equal, non-discriminatory wages; and innovative experiments in implementation, like the female mate system in Rajasthan, synergization of

MGNREGA with other schemes in Kerala and in Bihar, gender differential tasks for uniform (minimum) wages.

Slow implementation and the overall low level of job creation in states like Uttar Pradesh, West Bengal, and Bihar, household-based job cards and a household definition based on common kitchen, thereby causing exclusion of single, divorced and separated women are all factors that have restricted women's participation in some cases. The local socio-cultural factors also play a role. Women are subjected to discrimination at the level of household registration and in issue of job cards, including complete denial to single woman households in states like Uttar Pradesh. In most parts of the Hindi heartland, there is a notion among the upper caste landed communities that allowing women to work outside their home would amount to a loss of honour and dignity of the family. Apart from socio-cultural restrictions, the presence of contractors on worksites (which is not legally permitted), a schedule of rates-based wages and delays in wage payment and lack of childcare facilities have restrictive effects on women's participation as workers under the MGNREGA.

In Bihar and Jharkhand, the nature and capacity of local institutions and socio-cultural factors are the main reasons for low women's participation. First, the scheme has been implemented in the backdrop of an administrative and institutional set-up not considered very efficient and effective in public service delivery. Bihar has improved its delivery efficiency since 2004-05, but in a top-down manner, the basic character of grass-roots institutions: local bureaucracy and Panchayati Raj institutions (PRIs): has not changed much. On the other hand, Jharkhand is doing without formal PRIs; implementation by the bureaucracy in a centralized manner goes against the spirit of the MGNREGA.

Second, the demand for the MGNREGA job is confined mostly to SCs and OBCs in Bihar and SCs, STs and OBCs in Jharkhand. Most of these workers are landless with poor literacy levels, and face other economic deprivations. Local institutions are effectively controlled by a combination of landed upper castes and upper middle ascendant castes in Bihar. Following the 2006 panchayat elections in Bihar, the dominance of the erstwhile elite in local institutions has, however, declined. Similar problems exist in Jharkhand, where job seekers are unable to translate entitlements into effective demand, owing to the incapacity of local institutions. The problem is not unique to these two states.

Third, participation of women from upper castes is negligible and from OBCs it is limited. Due to social restrictions, upper caste women, even from poor families, have not come forward. The upper OBCs have some amount of land and women prefer to work on their own fields; while the lower OBCs, mostly service castes, have traditionally been dependent on Jajmani services, and vestiges of this still remain.

Even so, the emergence of women workers as independent bread-earners with control over their earnings has had significant empowerment effects, such as a greater decision-making role in the family, discretion to spend and control the use of their earnings, and confidence to earn independent of male family members. Moreover, reports of their increased participation in the gram sabha are encouraging, and might change the character of decision-making in democratic institutions at the grass-roots level, which continue to be male-dominated even after the increased representation of women following the 73rd Constitutional Amendment Act.

In addition, the study also aims to look into the broader concept of empowerment, and studies the family dynamics at play. This study attempts to analyze data based on the family size. The data has been divided into two sub-groups: those having family size of more than 5, and those having family size of up to 5. Women's needs are divided into practical and strategic. Practical needs are related to food, clothes, housing etc.; and strategic needs are related to long-term issues of developing the ability to change the position of subordination and discrimination. The MGNREGA aims at meeting practical needs of women workers in the short run and their strategic needs in the long run. Women are able to buy food, clothes, medicines etc., from their MGNREGA earnings that addresses their short-term needs. Their reduced dependence for these basic needs on male family members also addresses the issues like subordination and subjugation in the long-term.

Till recently intra-household dynamics and issues were considered outside the domain of mainstream economics that deals mainly with market institutions. Male-female intra-household relations are also defined by their differential bargaining power, and in turn, determined by their differential access to economic, political and social resources. Property ownership and access to paid employment opportunity outside the household, apart from other factors, increases the bargaining capacity of a woman by giving her a better fallback position. Since, in India and elsewhere, male family members have greater control over property and other economic resources, including access to paid employment, they enjoy better bargaining positions inside their households. Thus, women's ability to earn outside their households increases their own self-perception of their contribution to the household, and this has similar effects. The paid employment opportunity under the MGNREGA holds similar prospects for rural women in India, who have little control over economic resources, and face social and other disadvantages in accessing paid employment outside the home.

The present study takes a broader view of empowerment and defines it both as a process and as an outcome that alters the position of women both, inside and outside their households, in respect of their better individual and social life.

The effect of the MGNREGA on empowerment of rural women is evident. How has paid employment under MGNREGA transformed the (bargaining) position of rural women within their households? And to what extent have participatory development processes under the MGNREGA been able to create larger social effects on women's empowerment? The former has been analyzed at the household level and with respect to the following three interrelated processes and outcomes: (1) Income-consumption effects; (2) Intra-household effects (decision-making role); and (3) Enhancement of choice and capability.

The latter has been explained at the larger community-level and through: (1) process participation; (2) wage-equality and its long-term impacts on rural labour market conditions; and (3) changes in gender relations, if any, because of the above and other factors.

Women's contribution to household income and to national economy remains largely unaccounted for as they undertake a significant amount of unpaid work. To many, this remains a fundamental challenge of women's empowerment. A time use survey conducted by the Central Statistical Organization (CSO) across six states revealed that, on an average, rural women spent about 22.53 hours of their weekly time on System of National Accounts (SNA) activities and 33.95 hours on extended SNA activities. This, in fact, reiterates that the average number of hours spent by women on unpaid work is high and their contribution to the household's income and overall welfare remains unaccounted for and unappreciated. The MGNREGA has helped women in converting some unpaid hours of work into paid hours of work with significant effects, especially for those women for whom the MGNREGA is a primary work opportunity outside the home.

The study observes significant income consumption effects. This means an increase in the paid income of a woman worker and consequently her ability to choose her consumption basket. Though income and consumption are related, we emphasize consumption, because an increase in income sans the ability to consume or choose consumption baskets has little significance. For example, if a woman earns, but is unable to exercise any choice on how to spend those earnings and instead, say, surrenders her entire earnings to the head of the household, she does not influence the spending decision at all, and subsequently the element of empowerment is probably missing, in spite of the income effects. Paid work under the MGNREGA has helped rural women in realizing income-consumption effects through monetized earnings and better control over earnings because of monetized wages and account payment leading to better consumption effect.

Underlining the significance of paid work and its effect on the self-perception of women, a woman worker told the researcher in a lighter vein that now that she earns, her husband is ready even to prepare tea for her, something quite unlikely earlier. Some also said that when they hand over either part or whole of their earnings to the head of their households or to any other male family members, they feel a sense of worth and importance. Earning is important, but equally important is retaining and exercising choice over use of earnings. Sixty-eight percent of the women workers are collecting their wages themselves.

It appears that account payment leads to greater incidence of self-collection and control over wages. The high proportion of women, who collected their wages themselves, was in fact co-terminus with 100% account payment. On the other hand, in many of the cases, male household members collected women's wages, as cash payment was still in practice and often payment was made to the male household member on behalf of the household. The local social setup accepts the practice of the man collecting wages on behalf of female family members, as often a household is identified by the name of the head of the household. Local officials and PRI representatives easily cooperate with male members to earn their support and favour.

It was observed that sometimes women collect their wages, but hand it over either to the male head of their households or to their husbands. Sometimes, they retain a portion and surrender the rest. Nevertheless, self-collection increases the chances of retaining control over wages.

The majority of women workers were found to collect and retain their wages. Significantly, it was found that 55.6% of sample women retained up to 25% of their wages. The proportion of women who controlled up to 25 percent of their MGNREGA wages for personal use/consumption is estimated to be around 50 percent.

A large number of women, who retained either part or whole of their MGNREGA wages, also exercised choice over its use. They used it for all kinds of purposes on daily consumption items, household durables, health and education of children, visiting relatives, and on social ceremonies etc. They also used it to meet their personal needs. The most common items of personal need women spent on included clothes, cosmetics and bangles, personal health (medicines), visiting relatives and giving gifts at the time of marriage and festivals to near and dear ones.

Its significance lies in reduced dependence on male and other family members. Before the MGNREGA, 44% women said that they were able to meet their personal needs through their own earnings. Now, 71% women were able to do so. The pre-and post-MGNREGA difference is quite significant where the overall earning of women workers was relatively high because of greater number of person-days worked by them. It seems that women are able to spare for personal needs only when they earn a minimum income, as other priorities of the household are equally pressing. This also registers the significance of realizing a critical minimum number of person-days and wages for improved effect on women workers.

Interestingly, the majority of women workers, even after getting their own income through the MGNREGA, continue to receive money from earlier sources to meet their personal needs as per necessity and exigency. Of all women workers, around 70% continued to receive money from earlier sources. This underlines the fact that cooperation and understanding continue to play a role in household affairs in rural India, notwithstanding the bargaining model of the household.

The dominance of males in intra-household decisions in rural areas is unmistakable. As per the National Family Health Survey III (2005-06), only 29% of married women in rural areas take decisions about purchase of daily household needs; 26% decide about their personal healthcare; 7.6% take decisions about purchasing major household items; and only 10% decide on visits to relatives.

If we compare this with observed changes in the case of the MGNREGA women workers, the impact is remarkable. Now, 71% women retain portions of their income to spend as per their own choice. These relate to purchase of household items, healthcare, visits to relatives etc. Moreover, the domain of their decision-making has also widened. One woman worker in Kangra used her MGNREGA income for the construction of a toilet inside her house, and interestingly, this was her own decision. Many of these women are now able to visit their relatives, mostly their maternal homes more frequently. Earlier, their visits were doubly controlled by permission and money required for it. Additionally, a number of women workers had invested in fixed deposits for the sake of their children, something that earlier would have been beyond the domain of their decision-making.

The MGNREGA has broadened choices for rural women in several ways. One, it has opened for them an entirely new avenue for paid employment. Secondly, it has broadened their choices and capability as a result. An important fact is that a large number of women decided on their own to work under the MGNREGA. Thirdly, MGNREGA has increased the choice set for women by reducing economic dependence on other family members. When a woman worker depends on the head of her household, the latter's discretion limits the choice or indulgence of the former by amount and timing.

Paid employment under the MGNREGS has enhanced both freedom and the choice to use earnings. Women's participation in grass-roots community development processes in general, and decision-making in particular, remain weak in spite of their increased representation following the 73rd Constitutional Amendment Act. Apart from low participation in the gram sabha and other decision-making fora, the problem of proxy (men performing the role of women representatives) is frequently found to occur.

One of the latent objectives of the MGNREGA is to strengthen community development processes through grass-root institutions and to make decision-making at that level more inclusive and participatory. Women's participation in procedural aspects under the

MGNREGA, say selection and implementation of works, social audit, asset management etc., remains low, even though their participation as workers has surpassed the benchmark of 33% at the all-India level in all three years of implementation. The low procedural participation is a fact even in panchayats headed by women.

Procedural participation is important for the realization of entitlement. The first and foremost issue is to know one's entitlements and the process of realization. Most women workers were aware of the basic provision of 100 days of guaranteed employment. But the level of awareness about the details of provisions, including women-specific ones, was low and varied across districts. Women workers were better informed of those provisions that had already been implemented, either partially or fully and were least aware of those provisions that they were not availing of at all. Moreover, the level of awareness/information was generally higher in places where implementation was better and greater for provisions that were implemented effectively. Literacy was another factor. Women in Hazaribagh were better informed of most of the provisions, because of relatively high literacy rates. Social mobilization by civil society organizations is another factor that can overcome the handicaps of low literacy rates.

Women's ability to search for the MGNREGA job themselves is another indicator of process participation. But only 5.4% of women were found to have searched the MGNREGA job themselves, as in most of the cases the gram panchayat head and panchayat secretary/rozgar sevak were seen helping them in their search for jobs. The role of different agencies varied district-wise even though the role of gram panchayat head/panchayat secretary/ rozgar sewak was appreciable in two blocks of Hazaribag.

Women's participation in selection of the MGNREGA works and social monitoring, including auditing was almost negligible. They were hardly involved in the management of assets created, though such participation was important to derive lateral benefits from the assets. This happened even in the panchayats headed by woman pradhans.

An increased participation of women in gram sabha meetings has been a positive development. Forty-five per cent of them had attended gram sabha meetings held in connection with the MGNREGA. It seems that women's participation in the gram sabha has been increasing. In another study of six north Indian states in 2008, only 33% of male and female workers were found to have attended the gram sabha meeting. It seems that the holding of gram sabha meetings itself has become a more regular phenomenon in the post-MGNREGA period.

A large number of women also said they spoke at the gram sabha meetings, the number going to 73%. However, it was revealed that women speak mainly about the availability of jobs, wage payment and other related issues of personal interests, not on community interests like the selection of work, social monitoring etc.

More women now also meet and interact with government officials and PRI representatives. Forty-six percent of them had the chance to interact with government officials. This has larger effect in terms of increase in their confidence levels.

Before the MGNREGA, only 16% of women workers' households had an account in a bank or post office. Post-MGNREGA, 70% of these households have access to a bank or post office account. Moreover, pre-MGNREGA accounts were mostly in the name of male family members. Now MGNREGA rural workers have accounts in their own names. Since the government has given a direction for account payment of MGNREGA wages, it is likely to be universalized in other places as well. The Jan Dhan Yojana too has played a vital role in it.

Account payment of wages has also created some other positive effect. Apart from increasing the chances for greater control over earnings, it leads to cultivation of a saving habit. Initially, most of these workers used to withdraw their entire wages at one go. Gradually, they have started withdrawing as per their needs. This has an added advantage as women are able to save money from wasteful expenditure, if husbands or other male members tend to spend on items like liquor. Women were also found to invest in fixed deposit schemes in the same bank. Greater linkage of women with financial institutions is likely to trigger many individual and community-level social and economic effects.

Ensuring equal wages for male and female workers in the informal sector still remains a major issue and a challenge for gender equality. The MGNREGA has achieved it in some places to some extent. The group measurement system, social mobilizations including social audits, absence of contractors and practice of a daily wage system have helped in realizing equal wages for members of both genders. Realization of equal wages under the MGNREGA has significant implications for the rural labour market. If women are able to earn higher wages under it, there is probability that they would not be willing (or available) to work for less than what they are getting under the MGNREGA. The reduction in the supply of women labour force would create supply-side pressures on the labour market that would push up the wage floor. It was observed that many tea gardens in Kangra were finding it difficult to hire workers on the basis of their pre-MGNREGA wages. They had to increase the wages, and frequently this upward revision had to be done with consideration to the MGNREGA wages. Some of these gardens were on the verge of closure, as they were finding it difficult to operate at a profit with increased wage costs.

Subtle changes in gender relations have been observed but mostly at the household level. Increased say of women in decision-making, greater recognition of their contribution to the household income, and reduced dependence on male family members for meeting expenditures related to personal needs are some of those changes.

However, due to weak participation in other related processes at the same time, larger community-level effects yet remain to be realized. Even in the case of increased presence of women at the gram sabha, male participants dominate the decision-making process. Entrenched gender relations are hard to dismantle. While we were interviewing women workers in one of the villages, they refused to sit side by side on the cot in the presence of male members, as social norms prohibited them to do so.

Nevertheless, worksite experiences were enriching. Introduction of the female mate system has allowed women to reverse the role of a male mate/supervisor. For male workers, working under a female mate is a new experience. This may not change the character of gender relations immediately, but will have a definite impact in the long-run. Moreover, female mates were found to be more sensitive to the needs and requirements of women.

Working together gives women an opportunity to share grievances and personal problems, and helps them in development of women's solidarity. Women were observed to be exchanging help, for example, borrowing money and bartering goods among themselves for which they were earlier dependent on other people. Some old and physically weak women were found to be working on the sites. In spite of the group measurement system, nobody was complaining that these women were receiving the same wages, although their productivity was less. Rather, the group was considerate towards their old age and physical ability, and offered them easy and less strenuous tasks. In turn, some of the widows working at the MGNREGA worksites said that their coming out and working gave them a sense of purpose and belonging, compared to sitting at home and getting bored.

However, the MGNREGA benefits have not come easily: working hours for women have increased; their leisure time has vanished; and they have to bear with physical and emotional strains. They have to get up quite early to fetch water, prepare food and make arrangements for children before going to the worksite. Even during the official lunch break, some of them return home to take care of children and other family members. Wage payment is linked to a task-based Schedule of Rate (SOR), and since the SOR is prepared based on the average output of a healthy, invariably male worker, women have to work very hard to earn minimum wages. This is much more difficult for old, physically weak and lactating women.

In the absence of (proper) créche facilities, lactating women and women with young children leave their children at home while working at the worksite. Only 28% of the women with children under the age of five brought them to the worksite; 62% left their children in the care of siblings/elders; and another 10% of women left their children without proper care. Since, they have to remain away from home for a minimum of eight hours at the MGNREGA worksite, they remain anxious about the well-being of their children. Eighty-one percent confessed that they remain emotionally strained while they are working at the worksite and their children are left at home, either unattended or in another's care.

Modernity in Perspective: Conclusion of the Survey

There are three distinct but overlapping perspectives on women's development. These are Women in Development, Women and Development, and Gender and Development (WID-WAD-GAD). In fact, they have evolved in phases and in a chronological sequence.

Empowerment of rural women has emerged as an unintended consequence of the MGNREGA. Women have benefited more as workers than as a community. Women as individuals have gained because of their ability to earn independently, made possible due to the paid employment opportunity under the scheme. Independent and monetized earnings have increased consumption choices and reduced economic dependence. This has helped women in registering their tangible contribution to the household's income. The overall effect of these has translated into an increased say for women in household affairs.

Women as a community, however, have been slow in realizing the potential benefits of the scheme. Nevertheless, their increased presence in the gram sabha, the increasing number of women speaking out in there, frequent interactions with government officials and Panchayati Raj Institutions (PRI) representatives, and access to banks and post offices are new developments. Additionally, the female mate system has reversed the traditional gender roles, albeit in a limited manner.

On the flipside, working hours for women have increased; leisure time has vanished; and there are physical and emotional strains related to such work. Lactating women and women with young children work under emotional strain, as they remain separated from their children for long hours. Some adolescent girls are reported to have left their studies to avail of the job opportunity under the MGNREGA.

The challenges lie in horizontal and vertical expansion of benefits first. The high participation of women ensures horizontal spread of benefits. Realization of greater numbers of person-days ensures better individual-level effects. Districts with high SC and ST populations and states with high human and gender development indices and greater levels of state and civil society mobilization have benefited more. However, other than SC, ST, and OBC women, others are not forthcoming in availing this paid job opportunity.

Apart from implementation issues, there are social and cultural contexts that restrict women's participation in some places. Persistent social and community mobilization and a proactive role for the state can compensate for some of these social and cultural deficits. This will also be helpful in bridging the gap between work participation and process participation. Certain initiatives and changes can also prove helpful. The realization of sufficient numbers of person-days to earn a critical minimum income that triggers household-level effects is the first condition. Timely payment of wages through individual accounts of women workers encourages participation and greater control over earnings. A daily wage system, instead of wages as per the SOR, has been helpful in realizing minimum wages. The experience of Himachal Pradesh is proof of this and the Act does not prohibit it. Alternatively, a gender-sensitive SOR, as has been introduced in Bihar, can be experimented in other states as well. Working conditions need to be made more conducive by enforcing and strengthening existing provisions and adding new ones. For example, breast-feeding breaks for lactating women and flexibility in working hours may be considered. CrŁche provision may be linked with the Anganwadi or Integrated Child Development Services (ICDS) centres, panchayat bhavans, local school buildings etc., to make them more practical. Among others, maternity relief for women, along the lines of Maharashtra Employment Guarantee Scheme (MEGS), makeshift toilets at the worksites and innovations in work instruments so as to reduce work drudgery may be adopted.

Increased participation in procedural aspects and greater control over the types and management of assets can increase social and community benefits. In a state poverty eradication mission, setup by the Kerala government, it is organized into neighborhood groups of 15-40 households and each household is represented by a woman member. In terms of organization, it comprises an area development society (ADS) at the ward level and a community development society (CDS) at the panchayat level. The Kerala model of linking the MGNREGA with women's groups may be useful for greater process participation. A minimum representation of women among the MGNREGA functionaries like programme officers, rozgar sevaks, ombudsmen, members of vigilance and monitoring committees, mates etc., would be useful. Some of the assets created, if properly chosen, may reduce the load of unpaid work like fetching water, fodder etc. Creation of skill-generating assets like horticulture or fisheries through ponds can also be further explored to ensure better lateral benefits from such assets.

Long-term, sustainable development will only be possible when women and men enjoy equal opportunity to rise to their potential. Mahatma Gandhi firmly stated that the status of women would not change merely by bringing legislations; it must be supported by change in the women's social circumstances and situations and also men's attitude towards women. The MGNREGA, which entitles rural households to 100 days of employment on public works at the statutory minimum wage, contains special provisions to ensure full participation of women. It is a step in the right direction.

The MGNREGA plays a significant role to meet the practical as well as strategic needs of women's participation. It has become a beacon of light in the empowerment of rural women and has contributed substantially for the increased living and economic conditions by creating equal wages to male and female workers. It seems to facilitate the recognition that women's empowerment is an indispensable part of the development process. Indeed, it goes beyond the classic variables of empowerment and attempts to include 'the nature of the employment arrangements' emphasizes what Amartya Sen calls women's agency:

> [women remain] no longer the passive recipients of welfare-enhancing help, [but are] seen, by men as well as women, as active agents of change: the dynamic promoters of social transformations that can alter the lives of both women and men.[19]

□

4

Creating Wealth and Adding Assets

An important objective of the MGNREGA is creation of sustainable assets to strengthen the livelihood resource basis of rural areas. These productive assets are expected to generate resources for the alleviation of property and also create a sustainable resource for the next generations. Characteristically, with several inter-state and regional variations, its plan lists a wide range of permissible works. Since its inception, around 146 lakh works have been undertaken; of these, almost 51 per cent pertaining to water (water conservation, flood control, irrigation, drought proofing, renovation of traditional water bodies and micro-irrigation), and over 19 per cent to rural connectivity. At such a scale, the MGNREGA works have the potential to benefit rural communities by improving irrigation facilities, enhancing land productivity and connecting remote villages to input and output markets.

Quality and Durability of Assets

The studies pertaining to quality and durability of assets created by the MGNREGA have bordered on good as well as bad results. So, it has faced criticism on the quality and sustainability of the assets created under it. It is chiefly criticized for being labour-intensive, since employment generation is the primary objective of the Act. These works tend to be non-durable and have limited use. On the other hand, it is suggested that earthen works can also be durable if planned, designed and constructed properly.

Return on Investment/Cost Recovery

The expected return on the built asset is a point under consideration. Investment on the asset includes the initial cost of the structure as well as the payment made to the labour and other paraphernalia. A comprehensive study related to the MGNREGA works, conducted across eight districts of Bihar, Gujarat, Kerala and Rajasthan, is indicative of the productive potential of the scheme. It assessed 143 best performing MGNREGA water-related assets and found that the estimates are positive in the case of a majority of assets. Specifically, out of 143 assets, 117 assets had a return on investment of over 100 per cent in the first year, i.e., they recovered their investment in a single year of use. It was found to be 126 per cent for Gujarat, 121 per cent for Bihar, 101 per cent for Kerala, and 61 per cent for Rajasthan. Micro-canal systems were found to have the highest rate of return compared to all other MGNREGA works.

With renovation, water is available in these canals for up to eight months in a year and this has allowed the farmers to provide 3-6 additional irrigations to their paddy crops. It increased crop productivity by around 6-15 per cent, the bulk of the benefits for the farmers came in the form of diesel saving as they were able to replace costly well-irrigation. However, other studies indicate a longer recovery period for 100 per cent return. A study in Madhya Pradesh estimated that for similar assets (including ponds, wells), the recovery of cost period on an average was five years. This variation may be due to different methodologies followed for assessment as well as different geographic areas of evaluation. Factors like, the type of work being undertaken, technical design and the geological differences in areas of implementation are also crucial to determining the average recovery cost. Intra-state variation was apparent in the case of Gujarat where public assets created in Sabarkantha district were doing better than their counterparts in Junagadh in terms of economic benefits generated.

Perception-based Surveys

These surveys try to assess whether the assets are useful to the beneficiaries and are being used for the purpose they were created for. For these purposes, these surveys have been used to assess development utility of assets as perceived by stakeholders. In one of the survey rounds, in Andhra Pradesh, Madhya Pradesh and Rajasthan, it was found that around 99 per cent of rural households in Rajasthan, 82 per cent in Madhya Pradesh and 64 per cent in Andhra Pradesh were using the assets created through the MGNREGA works. Further, out of all the MGNREGA assets being used, 83 per cent in Rajasthan, 80 per cent in Madhya Pradesh and 67 per cent in Andhra Pradesh, were considered to be of good or very good quality. In yet another study conducted in five districts of Madhya Pradesh, 74 per cent out of 100 sample beneficiaries stated that the dug wells created under the MGNREGA had increased the total irrigated area and saved their crops from water scarcity.

Such positive outcomes have been reported in other parts of the country too. Research indicates that wherever village communities have taken enthusiastically to the idea of the MGNREGA and where their enthusiasm has been supported by an able, well-staffed administration and capable local governance institutions and leadership, results have been positive. In other instances, lags in process and procedure have reduced the efficiency of assets. A study conducted in nine states including Andhra Pradesh, Himachal Pradesh, Madhya Pradesh, Odisha and Rajasthan undertook a perception-based evaluation of 40 assets, such that seven best and seven worst works were selected. The assets were found to be of good physical quality and had followed most of the MGNREGA processes in timely wage payments etc. On the other hand, the seven worst assets had not followed the MGNREGA processes in terms of timely wage payments etc., and were of uneven quality; two assets were of moderate quality, two of poor quality and one was incomplete.

Technical Quality

Geographical location, feasibility, strength of physical structure and related aspects determine the technical design of an asset. Its sustainability depends to a large extent how sound its technical design is. A study was conducted with regard to critical design parameters under each category; for example, cost of investment, height, depth, technical design, quality of construction, time to recover the cost, among others. It was found that most of the structures, which were built under the MGNREGA, are sustainable and will last for their designed average life. This remains true of wells, check dams and anicuts, which have been found to be built with good-quality material and the right kind of technical inputs. However, it was also brought out that the durability of civil works on all-weather roads was low due to non-use of machines like road rollers.

Similarly lack of planning and careful execution could be seen in some projects like plantation. In a study in Jharkhand, the average life of plants was found to be only two to three years (as opposed to 15 and above years of productive life depending on the type of tree), due to lack of planning in selection of the location for these works as well as poor maintenance. In other places where plantation activities have been well-planned, saplings/trees were shown to have a high survival rate. These variations may be reflective of careful planning, execution and maintenance required for ensuring the feasibility and durability of works. Another study, which assessed ecological sustainability of the dug wells in Madhya Pradesh, pointed out that the technical design did not incorporate recharge facilities for these wells and thus the wells may dry up in the long run. In Andhra Pradesh, only 25 per cent of the 16 farm ponds were being utilized. This was because there was no provision for lining and that made the water percolate such that it was not available for supplemental irrigation. Nevertheless, in this case, the ponds were serving the purpose of groundwater recharge. Studies also indicate that in some instances, ponds are constructed without a conceptualization of the catchment area and recharge sources etc.

A research study in Rajasthan revealed that inadequate staff was a major reason for poor quality and effectiveness of assets. It noted that in Dungarpur district of Rajasthan, each technical assistant was responsible for supervising works in three to four gram panchayats, while in Tonk, a technical assistant was looking after works in 10–12 gram panchayats; a large number of MGNREGA assets in Tonk were rendered ineffective due to insufficient technical inputs in design and site selection.

A major weakness of water-related works under the MGNREGA has been the excessive concentration on excavation and desilting of ponds without corresponding work on treating their catchment areas or on the construction of dams based on earthen engineering.

Work Completion Rate

Work completion is an important parameter to evaluate the MGNREGA processes involved in creation of the asset, though it by itself is not a criterion to assess the quality of work. Out of 146 lakh works that have been taken up under the scheme (up to FY 2011–12), 87 lakh works have been completed, reflecting a completion rate of around 60 per cent. However, there is significant inter-state variation in the work completion rates. For example, Kerala recorded the highest work completion rate at 71 per cent, while the lowest was that of Maharashtra at 2 per cent. This remains a serious concern, not only because they fail to serve the purpose for which they were envisaged, but also loose soil from these works could potentially cause siltation of other water bodies in the vicinity. The important reasons noted for non-completion of ponds are found to be the following:

(a) In ponds, construction was not carried out according to planned dimensions; and
(b) Work on ponds was started in June–July before the monsoon.

Thus we see that there is deficiency in planning as well as technical design, which culminates into non-compaction of the soil leading to soil erosion and siltation.

Irregular flow of funds was another reason for incomplete works, as concluded by a study in Meghalaya and Sikkim. In Mandla, Madhya Pradesh and Narmada, Gujarat, a report found that while people started to work on the MGNREGA, due to delay in wage payments they shifted back to lower-paying works.

Lack of technical support to communities, on how to plan and when and where to start a work is also a key factor in non-completion of works. A large number of works, particularly those related to water conservation, remain incomplete, either due to lack of technical support to the gram panchayats or the onset of monsoons.

The Planning Commission set up a Working Group on the MGNREGA towards formulation of the 12th Plan, which suggests that works are left incomplete for several reasons, which can be variously addressed:

1. The Management Information System (MIS) needs to identify those works which are to be executed over a period of more than a year. Such works may be split into annual work elements, with each annual segment given a distinct work identity.
2. Some works are left incomplete because revisions of wage and material rates raise the actual cost beyond the approved estimates.
3. For delayed projects under execution, a survey re-estimating the value of the unfinished portion of the works should be carried out. The entire process of re-estimation must be done within a period of one month.
4. No sanction should be given for beginning new works under the gram panchayats where incomplete works have not been completed for more than one fiscal year after the year in which the works were proposed,

It is important to note that the findings related to quality, durability and rate of work completion suggest that the problem is not with the Act, but with implementation at the field level. For instance, lack of planning in areas like potential demand and need for the MGNREGA works, participation of villagers and prioritization of works in the gram Sabha, and focus on creation of productive assets based on principles of watershed etc., can greatly reduce the development potential of the scheme. Taking up of planned works, relevant to the need of the region and demand of the beneficiaries is also vital for ensuring ownership of assets and their development utility in the long run.

Work on Private Lands and Public Lands

The MGNREGA allows for asset creation, such as water conservation works, provision of irrigation facilities, land development etc., on public land. At the same time, it also provides for works, such as irrigation, horticulture and land development, on private land belonging to the Scheduled Castes (SCs) and the Scheduled Tribes (STs) or families below poverty line (BPL), or to the beneficiaries of land reforms or to those under the Indira Awas Yojana (IAY) of the Government of India or that of the small or marginal farmers as defined in the Agriculture Debt Waiver and Debt Relief Scheme, 2008 of the Government of India, or to the beneficiaries under the Scheduled Tribes and Other Traditional Forest Dwellers (Recognition of Forest Rights) Act, 2006.

So far as effective utilization of resources is concerned, a similar comparison may be drawn between creation of new assets and renovation of old assets. A study found that while creation of new assets was beneficial, investments in expanding, deepening, improving and renovating existing assets provided the highest returns; existing assets renovations had a return of 136 per cent, much higher than the return on new assets created which was 65 per cent.

The MGNREGA is demand-based, and taking up of one kind of work does not exclude the other. Still, there has been some debate on the effectiveness of works undertaken on public land in comparison to works on private land. Studies show that while private assets are preferred by beneficiaries, public assets benefitted a larger area and more people, leading to higher returns on investments. In a study across Bihar, Rajasthan, Kerala and Gujarat, 99 public and 44 private best-performing assets were surveyed. Of these, on an average, private assets recovered their investment cost faster. However, public assets are prone to destruction because of neglect in maintaining them, in the absence of strong local institutions: the classic tragedy of the commons. Community upkeep of public assets is limited, possibly due to ambiguity over ownership and usage rights. With defined ownership, assets on private land are relatively well taken care of and better maintained. This entails that development of private property under the scheme has the potential to contribute to more sustainable livelihood creation.

A study in Kerala observed that, of the 23 public ponds under study, only one was being maintained by the community; while in others, the villagers, including those who were directly benefited from the asset, asserted that it was the responsibility of the gram panchayat to regularly clean and maintain the assets. The possible reasons for the non-maintenance of these assets could be: diffusion of benefits over a large group and less individual ownership, disproportionate benefits accrued to influential groups, or weak Panchayati Raj Institutions (PRIs).

So far as the MGNREGA is concerned about reducing poverty, public works are prone to being taken over by interest groups (such as dominant groups based on traditional hierarchies, caste etc. These groups may, sometimes, block equal and open access to community resources like ponds etc. Thus, the choice between the two kinds of assets, public and private, in some cases, provides for a paradox between equity and effectiveness.

Varied Uses of MGNREGA Assets

Though most of the assets created under the MGNREGA are aimed at serving a single purpose, yet they are normally used for multiple purposes. Studies have shown that almost 50 per cent of the assets surveyed were designed for single-use, such as irrigation, but were de facto multiple-use structures, as they were also used for household purposes, groundwater recharge, livestock etc.

This reflects the potential of the MGNREGA to contribute to water and livelihood security in the village ecosystem. Each source of water, such as a pond, serves multiple purposes. Even within the homestead, households can use up to nine different water sources. This makes most of the water structures created under the MGNREGA multiple-use structures.

Thus in order to quantify the impact of MGNREGA and benefits accrued, it is important to take into account the nature and multi-utility of each asset. According to a field survey in Bihar, while ponds were demanded by the gram sabha primarily for purposes of irrigation, an important share of their benefits accrued were from pisciculture. Similar is the case so far as other projects are concerned.

The benefits from the MGNREGA assets in some cases can be directly measured, as with a quantifiable increase in the area irrigated, the storage capacity of a water body, the area afforested, the production of food, fodder or grass and other parameters linked to the functioning of the ecosystems. There are other uses and advantages of these assets that are more difficult to quantify; for instance, a study concluded that the MGNREGA activities reduced the vulnerability of agricultural production, water resources and livelihoods to uncertain rainfall, water scarcity and poor soil fertility.

Leveraging MGNREGA for Sustainable Development

The MGNREGA has opened up opportunities for convergence with different programmes, aimed at optimizing public investments made under existing schemes through suggested ways of linking and steering them towards a common/shared recipient end. To support convergence initiatives and allow for greater flexibility in adopting agro-climatic specific works, the revised

MGNREGA Schedules and Guidelines have added new works to the list of permissible works under the Scheme. For example, in Andhra Pradesh, effective convergence of the MGNREGA with horticulture was found. Under the state's Horticultural Programme and the MGNREGA, the cumulative area under mango horticulture plantations gradually increased from less than 30,000 acres in 2007–08 to more than 70,000 acres in 2009–10. Similar progress was seen in other areas too. In Madhya Pradesh, there is a convergence between the MGNREGA, agriculture and horticulture departments. The scheme provides water bodies for increasing water availability on the lands of farmers who have more than one hectare of land and belong to SC/ST and BPL families. It has resulted into an increase in water availability and crop yield.

□

5

Labour, Migration and Agriculture

Migration has been integral to the process of human civilization. Men's relation with agriculture and labour are concomitant to the process of migration. Migration has been forced upon people, as in the case of slavery under colonization, and nurtured development in certain civilizations, both agricultural and industrial. The migration of labour in India, especially those who are landless and work as foot-soldiers in the rural agricultural economy, has not been linear. The movement is largely fluid and dynamic with people flowing in several directions and into several occupations. Migration itself is rarely free from obstruction and exploitation. Not merely are the migrants subject to violent exploitations there are several emotional and psychological distress associated with it. For the rural, uneducated poor in India the choices of migration are also severely limited by cultural and social constraints. The MGNREGA has been enormously successful in addressing some of these problems. Not merely has it prevented the migration in its areas of implementation, it has also changed the relation of the population with the land they call their home.

The MGNREGA can be seen as an important response to the distress that leads to migration. As a commentator observes:

The difficulty of finding paid work, the sheer possibility of being duped, the exposure to criminality of various sorts, the problem of dealing with such basics as housing and sanitation, has been found[20] to lead to migration and makes it such a frail proposition for the migrants. The MGNREGA has greatly influenced rural labour markets and there are several dimensions to it.

It has been noted that MGNREGA affects not only the workers' lives but also works as a cushion to the family. Female migrants are migrating more frequently and in greater number than men, and that is creating, according to some observers a 'crisis of care' in rural India in particular and Asian countries in general.[21] The programme is not merely instrumental in dealing with this crisis by making the home more attractive and secure for women but also by ensuring employability for those who are left behind. It has resulted into expanded workforce as it has drawn in even those who were not active workers as it provided attractive and convenient work opportunities easily. At the same time, it is argued that the scheme has resulted into labour shortage in the other labour markets. It is natural for people, already engaged in the rural labour market, to seek the MGNREGA work if wages and employment conditions are better than their current employment, thus forcing the other employers to bring up their wages. It has had effect on migration too.

Impact on Agricultural Labour

Despite an argument favouring shortage in agriculture labour, it is seen that it is not caused entirely by the MGNREGA, such trends precede the coming into force of this scheme. Data from FY 2010-11 suggests that

70 per cent of the works in the scheme have been generated during the agriculture lean season. On the other hand, data from some studies demonstrate that there has been a change in the composition of the MGNREGA labour force where more agriculture labour is participating in the scheme.

There is, therefore, no conclusive evidence to support the claim that the MGNREGA has led to a shortage of labour in the agriculture sector or vice versa; however, the prescribed minimum wage for rural labourers has been considered to be a significant impact of the scheme, and those who do not want to pay it have felt the shortage for sure.

Shortage of Agricultural Labour

Let us first deal with the impact of the MGNREGA so far as agriculture labour is concerned. It is argued that government's hiring of unemployed labourers would affect labour supply across peak and lean agricultural seasons, thus having direct repercussion on wages and indirect effect on agricultural output.

The available data suggest that the MGNREGA has had a positive impact on labour force participation in public works. A study, comparing the MGNREGA districts and non-MGNREGA districts, has found that the probability of a casual worker being engaged in public works increased by 2.5 percentage points more in MGNREGA districts compared to non-MGNREGA districts. Similar results were seen in other studies.

Despite a large level of labour being employed under the MGNREGA, it is difficult to suggest that this casual labour in the MGNREGA is actually labour from the agriculture sector. The shortage in agricultural labour and their diversion from farms may be due to factors outside this scheme. In fact, post 2004–05, there has been a negative trend in labour force participation. The

National Sample Survey Organisation (NSSO) data indicate that this decline is also with regard to the agriculture labour force; thus, the decline in agriculture labour at the national level is since 2004, well before the MGNREGA came into force.

Different studies have pointed out that high non-farm wages, and not the MGNREGA, have had a more significant role in the diversion of labour from agriculture. Using macro-level data, it was seen that the impact of the MGNREGA wages on the economic scarcity of labour is more prevalent in Karnataka and Rajasthan which are drought-prone; however this impact is relatively modest when compared with the impact of hike in non-farm wages. The provision of food security through the Public Distribution System (PDS) has also contributed to the short supply of labour, the relative hike in non-farm wages is contributing to higher economic short supply. In other words, labour is being diverted away from agriculture due to more lucrative non-farm wages than the MGNREGA.

The study also indicates a powerful seasonal fluctuation, with a disproportionately higher share of works being done during the agricultural off-season. The month-wise employment data under the MGNREGA during FY 2010-11 indicates that it is in the lean agricultural season (April-June and January-March) that around 70 per cent of person-days of work were generated. While this does not factor in migration of labour during an agricultural lean season to other places, it does suggest that the impact of the MGNREGA on labour markets may be limited at best.

At the same time, the effect of the MGNREGA cannot be discounted from having influenced the supply of labour. Some studies have found a change in the composition of the labour force that participates in MGNREGA. A study, conducted over 1064 rural households in Andhra

Pradesh over two years, showed that in the initial years, the MGNREGA predominantly attracted non-agricultural labour (78 per cent), because participation in the programme was concentrated in the dry summer months when agricultural labour work was scarce. Over time, however, the programme was seen to be attracting households that would have participated in agricultural labour (55 per cent). This suggests that the MGNREGA is not just viewed as an employment assurance during slack agricultural seasons but also as an alternative to agricultural labour work.

The NSSO panel survey in the states of Andhra Pradesh, Madhya Pradesh and Rajasthan, observed that about 84 per cent, 80 per cent and 61 per cent were 'agricultural labour' households or 'self employed in agriculture' households respectively.

Taking synthesised results from different studies, we come to suggest that it is difficult to generalise the impact of the MGNREGA on labour markets and that the impact may vary from place to place. It is noted that the impact of the MGNREGA has been additive, expanding the labour market by attracting new labour to the workforce. However, the impact on agricultural labour cannot be denied.

The above impacts can be summarized as follows:

1. In places where the volume of the MGNREGA work is small compared to the demand and compared to the total size of the labour market, the scheme has no perceptible impact on local labour markets.
2. If there is a competitive local labour market, with several employment opportunities outside the MGNREGA, the latter offers limited scope to influence the labour market. In such cases, there was neither interest in the scheme's wage benefit nor in its non-wage benefit. If there is already

higher wage rate outside, why will anyone choose to go for the smaller wage?

3. The shortage in labour can be seen in places where the MGNREGA wage is higher than the local wage, and its presence is large enough to catalyse widespread interest in the community and also to significantly change the structure, conduct and performance of agricultural labour markets.
4. However, the MGNREGA, despite its higher wages, is not a source of attraction and will draw a lukewarm response if there are administrative constraints or there is lack of awareness among people, or both.

Thus, we can clearly see from the above analysis that the local labour market can significantly influence implementation of the MGNREGA works as well as people's participation in the scheme. The districts and villages which have adequately performed in implementation of the MGNREGA works demonstrate a visible growth in agricultural production, though this impact does not seem uniform.

Improved Irrigation and Change in Cropping Pattern

Water is a basic need for farming. The water-related assets created under the MGNREGA have increased the number of days in a year when water is available with improved quantity for irrigation. A study in Madhya Pradesh noted that 70 per cent of the irrigation structures under the Kapildhara Scheme ensured perennial water across agricultural seasons for beneficiaries. Availability of water increased from to 35 per cent in different areas. Increased availability of water has led to changes in crop patterns and increased area under cultivation. In a study, around 55 per cent of 240 respondents together reported an increase of 372 acres under crops. And around 56 per cent of the respondents reported diversification of crops over previous years. The crops like jowar, bajra, kodo, makka and arhar have been replaced by wheat, gram and vegetables due to increased availability of irrigation water. Similarly in Kerala, it was seen that due to renovation and construction of ponds and resultant improved water availability, commercial crops like ginger and sugarcane are being grown on a larger scale.

Increase in Crop Productivity

The MGNREGA has great impact on agricultural productivity following improvement in irrigation, land development, regeneration of natural resource base and large scale investment directly into the village economy. Districts and villages which have performed better under the MGNREGA works and used funds efficiently seem to demonstrate a visible growth in agricultural productivity. In a study of 640 households in four districts of Rajasthan and Madhya Pradesh, it was found that the annual growth rate of agricultural productivity of non-irrigated land has improved. In three districts, the average annual growth rate of agricultural productivity was positive and ranged from 1 per cent to 12 per cent across villages. This growth was directly attributed to the water-related works and structures taken up under the MGNREGA, since the monsoon in the years of reference was below normal (FY 2008-09). Significantly the growth in these areas was higher than the national average agricultural growth rate of 1.6 per cent for 2008–09.

This impact was higher in places where watershed development works had been undertaken. In Kerala, in an assessment of 40 ponds (25 public ponds and 15 private ponds) was made which were being used as secondary sources of irrigation. Their rice yields went up from 3000 kg/ha (hectare) to 4000 kg/ha, while coconut yields rose from 10,000 nuts/ha to 15000 nuts/ha. Another study in Bihar also revealed that renovation of these systems has led to improved water availability and irrigation for paddy, resulting into a 6-15 per cent increase in crop productivity. Similar results have been obtained from other states as well.

However, the impact of the MGNREGA on agricultural productivity is neither uniform nor conclusive, and more studies need to be undertaken, as improvement in agricultural productivity was reported in one area but not in others. Similarly, there needs to attribute change in crop yield, increased water availability for irrigation, increase in crop area, productivity of agricultural land etc., to the MGNREGA. Until such time, we should keep our fingers crossed, but with a positive set of mind, of course.

Increase in Bargaining Power and Choice of Work

The MGNREGA has proved to be a tool for the rural labour for bargaining on equitable terms. The wages under the MGNREGA provide an alternative source of income for rural labourers, raising the reservation wage (the fall-back position if a bargain is not struck) and implicitly offering labourers bargaining powers in an otherwise inequitable rural labour market. The scheme has also provided labourers (particularly those who are in debt bondage or contract labour) with a dignified choice of work. Thus, the diversion of labour may reflect an active choice made by the workers.

Providing Minimum Wage for Labourers

A positive impact for the entire range of rural labour is that the MGNREGA wages ensure an alternative source of income raising the minimum wage (the fall-back position if a bargain is not struck) of all workers and implicitly offering them some bargaining powers.

This must be seen as a positive development, since the Indian labour market, due to inequitable social and power dynamics, has suppressed wages far below the competitive wages for the rural labour force. For instance, in some areas, land-owners lock in or tie up labourers at a predetermined rate for agricultural seasons; but the MGNREGA has become impracticable in very many places. Many studies concur with these findings and further suggest that such benefits extend even to other workers who do not participate in the Scheme. Thus, the increase in average wage, whether agricultural or non-agricultural, is resulting in creation of more flexible and fair labour markets in rural areas.

Another field is the choice of work that the MGNREGA offers to rural workers. The agrarian relations in rural India exhibit a variety of labour hiring arrangements: from active casual markets in both seasons to tied labour/implicit contracts to collective bargaining between labourers and landlords. The explicit and implicit objectives of the MGNREGA target those labourers that are either involuntarily unemployed in the agricultural lean season or those that are desperate to escape the vicious cycle of poverty and debt. Thus, in places where there is a diversion of labour to the MGNREGA, the situation may just be indicative of an active and preferential choice made by workers. This choice of work is one of the arguments that find favour in demanding effective implementation of the MGNREGA in areas where contract labour/debt bondage still exist. Although there may be difficulties in making the switch from agriculture to the MGNREGA, the barriers need to be tackled according to the prevailing situation in an area.

Seasonal Availability of MGNREGA Works

There are fears that the positive effect of the

MGNREGA on agricultural productivity may be offset by a diversion of labour away from the agricultural sector. A study in Kerala has pointed out that the diversion of labour from rice fields may actually result in a decline in agricultural productivity.

Therefore, to limit distortion of the labour market during agricultural season as well as ensure that employment opportunities are additive instead of substitutive, there is need to schedule the MGNREGA activities during the non-agricultural peak season, in consultation with the gram panchayats, which can help to prepare calendars for the MGNREGA works. However, such scheduling may not be needed in the areas that have surplus labour that could not find employment even during the peak agriculture seasons; in which case the MGNREGA absorbs this labour. It also becomes a preferred choice for the labour under debt bondage, tied labour etc.

Migration

The chief cause of migration from village to town is search for livelihood; the other causes are not so prominent, which include medical treatment, higher education and urban facilities. Studies have indicated that the MGNREGA has reduced migration by providing work closer to home and decent working conditions to the workers in the former category, that is, those who migrate to look for livelihoods. Similar inferences have been drawn across different studies conducted to study this aspect of the MGNREGA. In many cases, it has drastically cut down the migration rates.

As per the National Census data 2001, around 15 per cent of the households migrate for employment. The impact of the MGNREGA may be more on the population that migrates for employment. In Punjab, while there has been a reduction in the in-flow of labour, as a large number of workers from Uttar Pradesh, Bihar, West Bengal and Assam seek employment there; while there is no significant impact of the MGNREGA on out-flow of labour from Punjab. This may be because, to begin with only a limited percentage of population migrates out of the state for only livelihood. In a study to assess the impact of the MGNREGA on migration in Punjab, it was found that only around 5 per cent of the 300 households in five districts reported migration from the village due to employment opportunities.

The World Development Report, 2009 contended that a reduction in migration, as caused by MGNREGA, is posing a barrier to internal mobility, thus limiting economic growth of these households. A majority of the studies on the subject note that the scheme has caused mostly a reduction in distress migration, and opportunistic or aspirational migration in search of better and more lucrative opportunities continues as before, particularly because the MGNREGA cannot match the wages of skilled labour in cities.

Reduction in distress migration may be more apparent in the case of households that need to migrate with their families, as all members are forced to migrate to cities due to limited work opportunities. This leads to disruption in children's education and access to family health care. A study across 12 districts of Gujarat, Madhya Pradesh, Maharashtra and Rajasthan, found that out of 938 beneficiaries, 55 per cent of the respondents felt that migration had been reduced in their families as a result of the MGNREGA. Thirty-five per cent of the respondents (out of 938 respondents) felt that their children's education had been positively benefitted by the scheme, while 30 per cent felt that their clothing had improved. The positive impact of the scheme has also been seen on reduction in child labour. As per the research, the MGNREGA has reduced the probability of a boy entering child labour by 13 percentage points and of a girl entering child labour by 8 percentage points. The MGNREGA also provides supplementary income for family members who choose or are unable to migrate.

The scheme also caused the labour market get vertically segmented: women, old people and the infirm sought employment with the MGNREGA and the able-bodied men demanding higher wages chose farm jobs. As a result, in many areas, most of the MGNREGA workers were found to be women and older men who were otherwise unfit or unwilling to migrate.

However, where the MGNREGA has not been implemented well, the reduction in distress migration has been reversed, such as in Mandla (Madhya Pradesh), poor implementation reversed the condition while it had initially reduced migration, mainly caused by delay in payment of wages. Thus, implementation is an important factor of the MGNREGA, and our next chapter will revolve round this aspect. While we cannot completely compliment the programme in this regard it has surely made advances that point to a more sensitive direction in the future. We must remember that

Distress migration for economic motives, although consisting of relatively short episodes, is now a perpetual feature of Indian society. Although it does contribute to macro-economic stability, it also imposes tremendous costs on those forced to undertake it. Policy-makers and the public need to become more sensitive to its manifold implications and take necessary measures to ensure that distress-led migration does not degenerate into further trauma.[22]

It is a challenge that requires a sensible and comprehensive response from both the planners and the future implementers of the MGNREGA. The challenge to innovations in the design of the programme will be in to ameliorate the negative spill over into the soil, the water, and from non-agricultural sector while sustaining growth in agricultural production. The capacity of the programme to coordinate these two sectors is immense. The MGNREGA has to play an important role in creating the economic environment in which agricultural production is to be made in the country and pool in all its resources which scatter fruitlessly through migration and discrete work.

□

6

Environment and Sustainable Development

No policy or programme undertaken in a developing or a developed nation can now afford to ignore the question of environment. Environment, defined in the large sense that includes both natural environment and built environment—'buildings and works, and the other modifications which the human race makes to the natural environment'—is at the centre of the global discussion on sustainability for a long time now.[23] Development must not merely sustain itself and establish a perpetual network of productive institutions. It must ensure that the environment and all its components are in mutual harmony and in a position to retain that balance for the long foreseeable future of humanity.

The global demand for agricultural production, especially for food, has reached an unprecedented magnitude and promises to continue to escalate well into the next century. Much of the growth in agricultural production will continue to come from increasing yields. And, as we have seen in the last chapter, MGNREGA is to play a substantial role in enhancing agricultural yield and in preventing the demise of agricultural environment caused by rapid industrialization in India's developing economy. Indeed, Prabhat Patnaik argues that the employment guarantee programme is also an ethical compulsion of government that is under an irrevocable pressure to embrace neoliberalization.[24] However, growth in demand, combined with unequal access to land and food, has extended the frontiers of agricultural production inexorably outward, raising concerns about the environmental wisdom and sustainability of major restructuring of agricultural land. The development project that claims only to touch land that is agriculturally fragile, marginal, or vulnerable must also make sure that the this land is not further deteriorated so as to disturb the ecological health of the planet. It is with this concern that many of MGNREGA work needs to be designed.

The MGNREGA is chiefly an employment scheme aimed at rural India, yet it has helped in augmenting ecological conservation. The Act aims to create sustainable livelihoods through regeneration of the natural resource base of rural India, furthering the cause of resilience and adaptation to climate change. Evidence of suitability of the MGNREGA works in terms of their usefulness for environment and ecology is emerging. In the short run, the works under the scheme provide environmental services aimed at natural resources at the local level, such as water availability, recharging groundwater, conserving water, increasing the area under irrigation, reducing soil erosion, increasing soil fertility, conserving biodiversity, reclaiming de-graded crop and grazing lands and carbon sequestration. When all these benefits are combined, they produce at a large scale, regional implications for climate change mitigation and carbon sequestration.

Now we shall focus our attention to project environmental and agricultural impact of the MGNREGA. It has had a positive impact at the micro-level, but studies are needed to assess it at the macro-level.

Environmental Services as Strengthened by the MGNREGA

The impact of MGNREGA works can be clearly seen in the rise in groundwater, improvement in soil quality and reduction in vulnerability of production systems to climate variability. Naturally, the extent and kind of impact the MGNREGA works have on the environment depends on the scale of activities being undertaken, their technical design, quality of assets created and ownership and use of the physical structures constructed. We have already discussed these points in the preceding chapters.

Several studies suggest that the MGNREGA has had a positive impact on the environment, but there is need to quantify it, so as to know it extensively. A pilot study was undertaken in Chitradurga, Karnataka for this purpose. Its findings have suggested that the potential and extent of impact depended on the scale, technical design, ownership and maintenance of the structures constructed and activities undertaken.

While effective planning is vital to ensure the usefulness and sustainability of the MGNREGA works, studies point that some of the works are easy to execute and can even be categorized as 'fail-proof'. In other words these activities can improve soil, water and forest resources without requiring micro-plans and watershed plans.

We can enumerate the impact of the MGNREGA works in the following table:

Renovation of Traditional Water Bodies: Improved storage capacity, irrigation availability, water conservation recharge, soil quality (nutrient cycling), biomass production and crop production

Water Conservation and Harvesting: Groundwater recharge, soil moisture retention and protection, water conservation, flood control, providing irrigation and drinking water and improving soil quality

Irrigation Provisioning and Improvement: Providing irrigation, improved-agriculture and livelihoods; reducing the need for methane increased crop production producing large dams

Land Development: Land reclaimed for agriculture, improved-irrigation availability, hence agriculture and livelihood improvement

Flood Control: Better drainage, higher land productivity and water conservation flood control

Drought Proofing: Soil moisture retention, protection of soil, water conservation, carbon quality, flood control, biomass sequestration, biodiversity production and local climate regulation conservation.

The above impacts can be exhaustive or on a limited scale, but their impact cannot be ignored in terms of ecological advantages.

Rise in Water Percolation and Groundwater

In the MGNREGA works that undertook projects on water conservation structures, desilting of traditional water bodies, plantations and other works have improved water percolation and helped to recharge groundwater. This has also led to a rise in groundwater levels and water availability, increasing the area under irrigation in some cases. An assessment of 34 anicuts was undertaken in Rajasthan; it observed that on an average, an anicut built under the MGNREGA was irrigating an area of 26 hectares and enhancing groundwater recharge for 3-25 wells leading to a rise in water levels between 10–40 feet. Similar experiences have been felt in other places. Results from a project in the Khargone district of Madhya Pradesh also demonstrate the collective impact of planned MGNREGA works on water and livelihood security. At the end of a three-year MGNREGA project (2010–12), on revival of a river (including desilting, check dams etc.), there was an increase in water availability such that the duration of the surface water level flow increased by two to three months, the groundwater level increased by two to three metres and the crop area increased by about 400 hactares.

Improvement in Soil Quality

The excavated silt from the MGNREGA works, if applied, has the potential to add to soil fertility. In a study in Chittoor, Andhra Pradesh, it was applied to 36,000 acres of degraded lands belonging to Scheduled Caste (SCs)/Scheduled Tribes (STs)/Below Poverty Line (BPL) families. This increased soil fertility in terms of nutrients found in the soil. Croplands that had been treated by silt excavated from water bodies, recorded a two to three times increase in the organic carbon content. The study conducted at Chitradurga has also confirmed this.

Potential for Carbon Sequestration

The above study at Chitradurga also attempted to estimate the potential of MGNREGA works to generate carbon sequestration, projecting the potential carbon sequestration over a period of 30 years, and it came to be enormous.

Reduction in Vulnerability of Production Systems

The MGNREGA works have resulted into reduced vulnerability of production systems to climate variability by strengthening livelihood and water security through water conservation, water harvesting and desilting and increased crop yields, as well as leading to an increase in water availability.

Creation of Dignified Green Jobs

The MGNREGA has helped to provide the rural

population with dignified works that are in conjunction with nature and greenery, so they have been described as green and decent. The scheme creates decent working conditions by ensuring that workers get their rights and legal entitlements, while providing social protection and employment. People are engaged in environmentally sustainable works that regenerate the ecosystem and protect biodiversity. Thus, the MGNREGA has helped to bring about a complete change in lives.

The MGNREGA creates dignified jobs which are decent and ensure productive and secure employment, social protection, rights, participation in planning; and are green in that they contribute to environmental sustainability, such as protection of the ecosystem, reliance on renewable sources of energy; and thus, they are directly related to climate change mitigation and adaptation activities.

In a pilot study in Bihar, six worksites were assessed in terms of decency of work such as days of employment against demand, wage payment, worksite facilities, employment to women and related issues. All of these worksites scored high. The specific findings revealed that (a) 100 per cent of the daily wage commensurate to the work done was paid; (b) 91-100 per cent of the days of employment demanded were provided; (c) Worksite facilities such as crŁches were not available at some locations; (d) All wage payments were made in 7-15 days; and (e) Employment provided to women was more than 33 per cent.

Decency of work also incorporates dignity and absence of harassment at the workplace. For instance, workers can be vulnerable to exploitation, illness etc., but the MGNREGA provides an opportunity for decent work. A field survey in six northern states found that workers regarded the MGNREGA as dignified employment. Ninety per cent of the workers reported no incidence of harassment at the workplace, it is largely seen as due to absence of contractors from the worksites. The workers too were found to be more aware of their wages and how much they should be paid. Thus, the MGNREGA is proving to be an effective tool for bringing about a change and rise of dignity among the rural population.

Yet, the programme has to respond well to the ever-widening agenda of concerns about the relationships between resource and environmental change, sustainable growth in agricultural production, and generation of rurally executable employment. The concern about the effects of more intensive coordination between agricultural production and non-farming supplementary work on resource degradation through erosion, salinization, and depletion of groundwater; and the quality of surface and groundwater through runoff and leaching of plant nutrients and enhanced use of pesticides among things are increasingly becoming urgent. Concepts that had initially been advanced by the populist critics of agricultural research—such as alternative, low-input, regenerative, and sustainable agriculture—have now become important part of the generative policies of agriculture in India. MGNREGA, as a support programme that works on the basis of small periods must pay attention to the. It is this broader agenda of negotiating the technical, environmental, and health constraints while answering the needs of growing employment crisis that must be kept in mind by the planners. The programme must, at every stage of its implementation, have inbuilt institutional mechanisms to take into consideration the possibilities of the loss of soil resources due to erosion, water-logging and salinization, groundwater contamination from plant nutrients and pesticides, and growing resistance of insects, weeds, and pathogens to present methods of control. Moreover, in heavily forested states like Jharkhand if industry and agriculture continues to expand into more fragile environments, such problems can be expected to become more severe. Additional deforestation will intensify problems of soil loss and degradation of water quality and will contribute to the forcing of climate change. The challenge lies in making MGNREGA actively sensitive and responsive to these challenges. □

7

Implementation and Governance

Jean Dreze and Amartya Sen ascribe some of the challenges and failures of MGNREGA implementation and governance to a 'worrying fatigue factor'[25]. According to them if this crisis is not overcome soon the programme is 'likely to be gradually reduced to a lame top-down scheme, instead of a demand-driven, rights based programme as it was envisaged.'[26] However they also point out to the enormous scope of operational innovations for further qualitative and quantitative growth of the programme. It is to these issues of fatigue and stagnation in policy and to the challenges in innovations that this chapter is devoted.

So far as proper implementation of the MGNREGA is concerned, we can classify the problems into different aspects in order to understand it in proper context.

The State Machinery and its Response tO MGNREGA

The issues and challenges faced by Government, so far as related to the implementation of the MGNREGA, are discussed below:

1. Honing the Skills and aptitude of the State's Representatives: For any programme of the scale and implications of MGNREGA to be successful, a judicious and active response of the people who implement vital. These people, in this case, are also not strictly people under the State but include representatives of civil society whose duty it is to keep the habit of consistent self-criticism and reappraisal on vigil. Such exercises have been, involving both the State and the Central governments and the numerous NGOS concerned with it, frequent in many territories where MGNREGA has been implemented well. These have clearly indicated multiple steps that can be taken for a better utilization and more effective planning of the enormous budget of the MGNREGA. The annual budget of the programme is about 33000 crore rupees, an amount which, the report by the Comptroller and Auditor General (CAG) of India cautions, must be used very systematically. It has highlighted the lack of administrative capacity of the village panchayat members to run this scheme in a designed and de-centralised manner. Indeed beyond some panchayats in West Bengaladn Karnataka, most local governance bodies in Indian villages are not inept in planning large-scale programmes.

2. Returning to the Objectives: Though MGNREGA was planned with a large, all-encompassing vision about the entire rural economy and environment in mind it is difficult to sustain the same focus and wide angled view of the programme at the site of its operation—the Indian village. For example the Act referred to conservation of natural resources such as rainwater, land, forests: an idea that viewed from the very narrow perspective of the village is not entirely visible. Thus, one can see that it is not reflected in the works floated for the scheme. Similarly, under this scheme, manual work has to be preferred and labour intensive projects need to be designed. Use of machinery and contractors go against the spirit of the larger objectives of the programme. The erroneous reports from the sites also often conceal the violation of the fundamental principle of the programme. Clearly, the objectives of the plan have not percolated enough down to the operational sites of the programme. This must be urgently addressed.

3. Dearth of committed manpower: At the block and gram panchayat levels, especially at the level of programme officer the programme requires two levels of workers, techno-managerial and administrative. Serious attention has not been paid to the former so far and as a result technical assistants, employment guarantee assistants, liaison personnel and other managers of the vast human resource in the villages are absent from the scene of MGNREGA employment. Another issue is inadequate number of administrative manpower in the field. This had led to burden on the existing machinery of the state and also caused the work to suffer. It has adversely affected the preparation of plans, scrutiny, approval, monitoring and measurement of works, and maintenance of stipulated records at the block and gram panchayat levels. In absence of these, as even the CAG report mention, the implementation of the programme has not achieved a desirable level of transparency.

4. Addressing the prevailing asymmetry in the society: The most remarkable feature of the MGNREGA is its unique and even accessibility to people from rural India without any discrimination on grounds of caste or gender. In some states, the powerful groups among the workforce get a large number of job cards. The scheme pays women the same as men, a phenomenon that was unimaginable in rural India even a decade ago. However, cases of discrimination against women and people from backward groups are reported from several regions of the country. Some states, such as Kerala and Andhra Pradesh, have registered a high percentage of women workers getting enrolled in the scheme, whereas others have registered a very low percentage of women availing benefits under it. Women are sometimes told that manual labour under the MGNREGS is not meant for women and they could not participate in ongoing works as it entailed digging and removing soil. The deeply entrenched patriarchal mind-set of the village society still determines gender based allotment of work in the MGNREGA jobs. So, we see reports that when the applicants are women only a few job cards are issued. In other cases there are indirect practices of discrimination like delays in the issue of cards for women applicants.

5. Need for a sustainable and dynamic fund generation for the scheme: The MGNREGA was started with an initial outlay of Rs. 11,300 crore in the year 2006-07 (almost 0.3% of GDP) and now fully operational, the annual budget for 2010-2011 was about Rs. 40,000 crore. This is one of the largest initiatives of its kind in the world witnessing manifold increase in all its dimensions in recent years. The total outlay for the programme has significantly widened every financial year. Some experts anticipate that the programme will end up costing 5% of GDP. Improved tax administration and reforms may create a larger pool of fund for the programme. At the same time the contribution of the scheme to the nation's productivity must be both enhanced and acknowledged.

6. Corruption and Irregularities: Former Prime Minister Rajiv Gandhi had once said that out of every 100 paise allocated for public welfare only 14 paise reached the targeted people, and this was true of this grand scheme too. Statistics suggest corruption has been a deadly hindrance to poverty alleviation in Indian and has ensured that these programmes have only a minimal effect on poverty levels in the country. The actual funds that reach the beneficiaries are very little compared to the funds allocated for welfare schemes.

Further concerns include the fact that corruption in the local governments leads to exclusion of specific sections of the society. Local governments have also been found to claim that more people have received job cards than people who actually work in order to generate more funds than needed, to be then embezzled by local officials. There are several cases of fake muster roll entries, overwriting, false names and irregularities in job cards. Even the names of dead people who have not registered often appear in the muster rolls. These are clear examples of how corruption has not merely led to absurd situations but also been of great damaging consequences to the implementation of fundamental rights under the Indian constitution.

7. Maoist/Left Wing Extremism Insurgency: The scheme is aimed at removing the disparity of living conditions in India that afflict our rural society at its most extreme. This is also the avowed vision of the supposedly left wing organizations which have spread their roots in the villages. The data shows that less than 9% of households in 60 districts most affected by Maoist militancy/left wing extremism found the required 100 days of employment under the country's rural job programme in the year ending 31 March, 2012. The national average of households that have completed 100 days under the job guarantee plan last fiscal was also poor at 10.1% compared with 8.8% in the districts hit by the Maoist insurgency. The percentage of women employed under the programme in the insurgency hit districts in the same period was 44% compared with the national average of 48%. The poor performance of the scheme in these areas has prompted the Rural Development Ministry to boost implementation of social and economic development programmes in the 60 Integrated Action Plan (IAP) districts in nine states, including Odisha, Jharkhand, Chhattisgarh, Bihar and West Bengal.

8. Lack of Safety Measures: The modern sensibilities have been profoundly altered after women's work outside the domestic sphere has been recognized as a vital component of human civilization. India is no exception and we have several policies for making the workplace more conducive for women. The rural economy has also constructively affected by these new demands of gender justice and, MGNREGA, which has one-third its stipulated workforce from the female sex must pay complete attention to it. Therefore, crŁches have to be set up so as to enable women carry their children to the worksite to do their work without much worry for their children. It is seen that women workers lay their children in cradles tied around tree branches. In the absence of this facility, women may hesitate to come forward to make demand for work and one of the objectives of the scheme to strengthen women empowerment may go unrealized.

Secondly, there must be a first-aid box available at the worksite to provide medical assistance to the needy workers in case they get injured during work. Importantly, life-saving medicines must be kept at the worksite because workers may get bitten by poisonous reptiles while clearing bushes.

Issues and Challenges Among People

1. Information and Awareness: The democratic impulses behind MGNREGA scheme can only be responded to by its potential beneficiaries when the exercises under the scheme become part of their everyday consciousness and awareness. A basic fact like the scheme provides the rural poor a right to demand work for 100 days in a financial year includes the idea of a right and hence is connected with the other rights in modern democracies, most importantly the right to be informed. The entire effort will be stymied if the governments do nothing to encourage people to know and register their demands. The fact remains that the national average for workdays generated under the scheme is less than half of the entitlement of 100 days per household/per year. Even in 2009-2010, a severe drought year, only 54 days of work per household was generated. In 2010-2011, this number decreased to 46.79 days. Due to lack of awareness about the provisions of the Act, people are unaware of their basic entitlements under the MGNREGA, such as job cards, minimum wage amount and unemployment allowance, and also about the receipt of application which is the basic record for claiming unemployment allowance. There is widespread ignorance about how to avail the unemployment allowance. Tendencies of the officials to suppress information about the specifics of the scheme arising from their fear of punishment for not providing jobs indeed amounts to gross violation of human rights. Additionally, poor awareness leads to corruption as well as poor management of the scheme; this is how the true potential of the MGNREGA is not being realized. The government must carry out an intensive training and awareness building programme to make the concerned officials and citizens fully aware of all the details of the programme. People at the grass roots level must be made aware of RTI Act and be encouraged to use it. It must be remembered that in a complex society like India no right can be implemented in isolation and each right is meant to complement the other right.

2. Disoriented Spending and inaptitude for savings: The MGNREGA has obviously increased earning capacity of the rural people. This, however, has not been translated into a creative orientation of their spending practices. These spending habits are of multiple consequences both for the workers and for the economy. For the workers it is important to conserve some saving out of the wage earned from the scheme. For example, payment to the workers under it is made in cash in Tamil

Nadu instead of through bank or post office accounts. Raw cash in hand leads to non-purposive spending on the part of people. Lack of awareness about the impact of inflation and illiteracy among the rural poor are the reasons for not saving part of their income from this scheme. In some cases, male workers have the tendency to spend considerable portion of their earning on drugs and liquor and the like. Therefore, the chance of creating financial inclusion is absent and the idea of saving is wiped out of the minds of the rural poor.

A sensitive planning that can reorient and capacitate the worker to spend the earning from the scheme needs to be envisioned.

3. A workforce without organization: In a constitutional democracy collective action for demands, restitution of rights and resistance to unjust and discriminatory practices are of utmost political and social value. Despite clear definitions, MGNREGA workers form a large amorphous body without any central organization. Given the floating nature of the involved population and the purely temporal nature of work, they fail to take collective initiatives in their own interest. A large number of extremely favourable provisions under the MGNREGA remain sentimental discourse of idealism but fail to be translated into actual material entitlements, for the workers. Being dispersed and disorganized works to their disadvantage and many a time they fail to get work for the stipulated 100 days, unemployment allowances and basic amenities at the worksite, among others. Dwindling demand for works under the scheme has eventually led the Jharkhand state government to promote the formation of unions of workers in the hope that this will persuade people in villages to ask for more work. Though the laws regarding these unions are still not very clear one hopes that will help in streamlining village planning processes and coalesce the local movements for political rights with the demands for economic and employment benefits.

Other Operation Glitches

The national average for employment days under the scheme falls wells short of even half the defined target. The average varies across different regions and states but the overall average is less than fifty days for the whole country. This, as we mentioned earlier, is a result of several policy and operational glitches that the scheme faces. They must be identified soon and addressed according to their impact on the implementation if the scheme has to contribute to the creation of strong and sustainable livelihoods for the poor in a truly meaningful manner. In addition to the operational problems, some of which we discussed above, some other issues need to be addressed too. The most glaring of all these issues, in my conviction, is to ensure an equitable and emancipatory participation of women under the scheme. In the following section I discuss some of the ways in which this can be done.

Improving Women's Participation in the MGNREGA

Women's work at any level in a patriarchal society is determined by a number of factors. In her classic work on women and land in South Asia Bina Agarwal sums up some of them in words that evoke the gendered background for MGNREGA workers equally well. The complex set of factors, to use Agarwal's words include:

> ...the continued assumption in most public policies of gender congruence in interests within family; the dominant view that men are the breadwinners and women the dependents; strong male vested interests in all land...; gaps between central government's

policy directives and the shape these are given at the state/province level...[27]

One can add to this list the complications arising out of the temporal nature of women's health and bodily debilities concerning certain kind of work, maternity roles, the burden of domestic and household work. A combination of these serve to point at the pessimistic and passive subject position of women as recipients of MGNREGA doles instead of wages. Several reports have conclude that women do not often take initiatives in finding work under the scheme and yet they find the work attractive and work without much vigour and much demands under it.

There are several reasons why women like the MGNREGA work. The primary feature that makes it conducive for women's choice is that it is locally available work that does not disturb the equilibrium between their domestic and occupational demands. The Act provides work within five kilometres of the residence of a worker, making it feasible for women's participation. Working at a distant place is difficult for women who happen to take main responsibility of household chores. Secondly, being locally employed gives a woman a sense of security and makes her less vulnerable to possibilities of exploitation. The principles of 'equal pay for equal work' and of guaranteed minimum wage form the bedrock of the schemes frame of justice and non-discrimination. It provides for a statutory minimum wage and which in most cases is much higher than that given by a private employer, more so in backward areas. The piece rate wages and formation of small and mixed/solely women groups have given leverage to evolve their working norms to suit their conditions. These factors instil in women a confidence in the MGNREGA scheme. Thirdly, there are regularity and predictability of working hours. As such, not only the members of the existing workers group, but also the new entrants prefer the MGNREGA work helping to expand the groups. Again, work is limited to eight hours a day, which is seldom expected in other works.

MGNREGA work has the potential to prevent migration of women. This leads to an improved quality of life located at a fixed physical site with emotional and material investments that multiply with contribution by other members of the family of the MGNREGA worker. The prevention of costs and risks associated with migration also adds to the emotional well-being of the women and helps them look after their kith and kin suffering from severe ills. Moreover, women can avoid harsh working conditions and hazardous works at private workplaces. These factors are responsible for the large number of women who are keen to get into the MGNREGA work. The national level consolidated figure, during the financial year 2008-09, shows that out of total labourers, 47 per cent were women. During the year 2009-10 (six months), the percentage of women's participation was 51. It indicates that the MGNREGA is fast feminizing the work force.

Implementation processes are key to improvement in the quality of participation of the marginalized, especially the poor and women in the programme. Gender sensitivity of the delivery system has a major role in motivating women wage-seekers for participation. Women functionaries in the MGNREGS are also expected to influence participation of women in a positive way, as it is assumed that women tend to respond more quickly to the needs of other women. Action towards women's needs, access to resources and opportunities, control over outputs and outcomes are essential.

Women's empowerment through MNRAGA has to be understood as a double edged process; it is both process and an outcome of the process that mutually reinforce each other. Enhancing women's agency, bringing them greater control over material and intellectual resources, and situating them at the creating cross currents of the manifold development programmes Empowerment is a dynamic but slow process; it will take a long time to bring changes in women and particularly from those among poorer households. During the last two decades, a number of development interventions, such as social mobilization, formation and networking and capacity building of women self-help groups have been put in place to empower women, and the MGNREGS is one out of them. However, active participation of women in any programme is a pre-requisite for their empowerment. Before I conclude this section let me add two suggestions that may be implemented for improving women's participation in the programme:

1. **Separate Accounts for All Job Card Holders:** There are instances where women in the job-card-holding households are either part of a joint account or not even featuring in any account at all. This practice should be completely discontinued and all women in such families must have their exclusive bank accounts. This single activity itself would probably ensure substantial progress in tapping the contribution of women who, although working in the field, are not being reflected in the musters.
2. **Creation of Facilities Specific to Women:** The MGNREGA has several gender sensitive features that are attractive for women workers. It stipulates that priority shall be given to women. In terms of implementation, it mandates that a minimum of one-third of the beneficiaries are to be women who have registered and have requested for work (Schedule II, Section 6 of MGNREGA). The state is obliged to ensure certain worksite facilities to enhance women workers' participation. The Act

also stipulates payment of equal wages to male and female workers. Wage earnings of workers are to be paid directly to the person concerned either through bank or post office savings account. In fact, the MGNREGA has opened up a new opportunity for women workers.

MGNREGA and Governance

In the last few years developing countries falling within the new regime of global capital and enhanced skill based employment have exceedingly been stressing upon the centrality of governance in their visions. It would be pertinent here to look at the standard objectives and methods of governance and evaluate the internal governance of MGNREGA and its external relation with the overall governance of the country. An extremely relevant description of governance comes from the UN High Commissioner for Human Rights. It deserves to be cited at full length for our purposes here:

Governance is the process whereby public institutions conduct public affairs, manage public resources and guarantee the realization of human rights. Good governance accomplishes this in a manner essentially free of abuse and corruption, and with due regard for the rule of law. The true test of "good" governance is the degree to which it delivers on the promise of human rights: civil, cultural, economic, political and social rights.[28]

The World Bank defines 'good' governance as 'sound development management' and emphasizes on its role in the relief of poverty.

The MGNREGA marks a radical departure from earlier wage employment programmes in terms of its legal and human rights driven framework. The cornerstone of its principles are taken from the constitution intention of securing social and economic justice thus making it ideologically congruent with the most loft visions of governance. However, when it comes to ensuring a system and delivery mechanism which is, in the words cited above, 'essentially free of abuse and corruption' there is no denying the fact that its implementation suffers from serious lags between theory and practice. This is a consequence of the complete failure in infusing the system with the new culture of demand-driven, rights-based, decentralized decision-making. In general, implementation of the MGNREGA in a state can be expected to depend on the quality of governance. States with better systems of governance and administration are more likely to have the ability to run complex programmes more effectively. On the other hand, poorer states have greater demand for work under the MGNREGA. However, they also have higher rationing rates and greater unmet demand for work. This is perhaps because their institutions are less capable of promoting good governance and suffer under undemocratic social structures that remain untouched by the rights-oriented legal environment in other areas. There is a possibility, therefore, that poorer states might end up in a vicious cycle in its implementation. They have higher demand for work but a less capacity to implement the scheme effectively and end up with greater unmet demand for work.

The other pertinent points pertain to low participation of women in some states, low capacity of gram panchayats, low quality and durability of some assets, low work-completion rates etc., which account for this; we have discussed these in the preceding pages.

Some of the major governance and process issues pertain to the initial stage of planning, demand for work, implementation at worksites, wage payments etc., as identified by independent evaluations. It also includes findings from a preparatory phase audit conducted by the Comptroller and Auditor General (CAG) of India. It is important to note that several states took action on the findings of the CAG and introduced systems to prevent procedural deviations and promote transparency in implementation of the scheme. In fact, when applied, the audit found improvements in record maintenance. Over the last few years, based on these reports from the field, the MGNREGA has instituted several reforms and policy changes in its implementation.

Awareness and Planning

The indifference among potential beneficiaries about certain provisions of the MGNREGA is largely a symptom of the poor informational traffic at the level of local self-governance. After more than a decade of panchayati raj institutions in the country we have still not been able to free them from the local moorings, concentrated information bases, and the inertial of social activism. This severely diminishes the ability of the rural poor to benefit under the Act. Infrequent meetings and low participation at the gram sabhas, and their persistent subordination to the dominant bureaucratic modes of governance from a distance has led to a limited implementation of the scheme at the village level in many places.

Awareness about the provisions of the Act is vital for the prospect beneficiaries. Studies have indicated that awareness levels among the potential beneficiaries about provisions of the Act, such as demanding work, unemployment allowance etc., are still low. The specificities of this ignorance reveals many fault lines in the governance of MGNREGA.

A National Sample Survey Organization (NSSO) panel survey on the MGNREGA, conducted in Andhra Pradesh, Rajasthan and Madhya Pradesh, in 2010-11 had discovered three aspects of the ill-informed target population:

(a) There is a substantial section of rural poor

who have little awareness about unemployment allowance.

(b) Most people did not know about the provision of work on demand under the scheme. The lack of awareness about the demand to work at any point in the year had a negative impact on the occupational planning of the poor.

(c) There is a very poor understanding of grievance redressal mechanisms, which result in a collapse of the right oriented, citizenship constituting programme of the Act.

Planning at the Gram Sabha and collective internal bargaining

The MGNREGA has huge pedagogic value in training citizens at the rural level. Deeply intertwined as it is with the economic interests of the people and since the local democratic bodies have been mandated to define, allot, select and prioritize the work it is natural that it will train the rural poor into acts of reflecting on their interest. Contrary to the individualistic tendencies that are supplanted by the movement of global capital, MGNREGA promotes exercises of collective bargaining. The MGNREGA is supposed to activate the democratic instincts of these people. It ensures that the development needs of each village are addressed through active participation of the villagers. The Act also prescribes that works be allotted in a way that at least 50 per cent of the total works (in terms of costs) be undertaken by the gram panchayats. This is to provide the groups a substantive role in their implementation.

The infrequent holding of the meetings of Gram Sabhas, low participation in the democratic procedure therein and the lack of compulsory imposition of decisions takes there have limited the way to accomplishing the vision of MGNREGA discussed above.

Rationing of Demand for Work

Rationing also exists with regard to households that would have liked more days of work but still had fewer than the 100 days stipulated by the Act. The NSSO survey does not take into account this aspect. However, it outlines some of the reasons for work not being available:

(a) The work was not available.

(b) Or, the worksite was not open.

(c) Or, work was not available even though the worksite was open.

There seem to be enough reasons for the local self-governance bodies to intervene in these matters and help the MGNREGA administrators identify the work. If possible these should be identified well in advance and a running record of potential worksites should be maintained at the level of the Gram Sabha. The scheme is based on the recognition that the beneficiaries themselves are in the best position to identify the work that must be done.

Demand for Work and Unemployment Allowance

The utility of MGNREGA work is not merely in the wages it earns for the workers but also in the psychological fulfilment of their demands and in initiating a chain of work demand that will eventually turn the village into a self-contained economic zone in many regards. The NSSO data note that around 19 per cent (June 2009 to July 2010) of the rural households sought but did not get employment under the MGNREGA. This could be due to a conscious stopping of works by state governments during certain seasons, among other reasons. Also there may be discrepancies in the scale of rationing as projected by the NSSO data. Nonetheless, rationing of demand greatly undermines the poverty alleviation potential of the scheme. Non-provision of dated receipts and work within

15 days and non-payment of unemployment allowance are other major process constraints.

The rationing of demands, thus, should not be based only a mechanical and arithmetical calculation of work and its monetary translation into wages. What is needed is an integration of demand with an accurately designed frame of social and political references.

Meeting Demand Accurately

As per the provisions of the MGNREGA, an adult member of any rural household, who demands work, should be provided work. However, it has been seen that due to low awareness, this does not happen due to limited capacity of the delivery systems and traditional social structures. In other words, there is a rationing of demand; households that are willing to work and seeking employment are not being given work. The rationing rate varied from one state to another. A study analysing the NSSO data observed that some of the poorest states, Bihar (34 per cent), Odisha (29 per cent) and Jharkhand (28 per cent), have low participation rates and high levels of unmet demand. This poses a paradox for implementation since these are the states which arguably require effective social safety nets for the poor the most.

The higher rationing in these states may be due to:

(a) Larger proportion of demand in these states to begin with.

(b) Low institutional capacity to administer the scheme that cannot match this demand.

(c) Lower levels of awareness and empowerment.

(d) Weak PRIs, which have a key role to play in the MGNREGA implementation.

It was seen that rationing could also be caused by a deliberate stopping of works during certain seasons by state governments. The local governments start and stop works throughout the year, with most works concentrated during the first two quarters of the year prior to the monsoon. The monsoon rains make construction projects difficult to undertake. Some studies point out that there may be interest groups influencing rationing and limiting participation. This is a vexed problem of working at any local level since the decision making is often circumscribed by the pre-existing power structure of the society. This is one of the pitfalls of any social upliftment plan that has to eschew the common route of competitive tendering and works with a faith in the beneficiary's own discerning abilities.

Dated Receipts

The Act clearly stipulates that every household that applies for work is to be issued a dated receipt. This receipt becomes the instrument for ensuring that the household gets work within 15 days from this date. Thus, this provision is vital to ensuring social security of the poorest. However, findings suggest that this is not always the case. It has also been figured that only 57 per cent got dated receipts while around 71 per cent got work within the prescribed period. Studies from other states have similar findings suggesting that dated receipts are often not issued.

Like, rationing, it is difficult to verify whether a household has been issued a dated receipt since application for work can also be made orally, in addition to the written form. This is again one of the persistent problems which can only be resolved by creating effective and transparent mechanism of job distribution.

Unemployment Allowance

An interesting conundrum that MGNREGA embodies is the double social security network of its existence. At a larger theoretical level the program itself is an extension of the social security principles of modern democracies which include benefits, not usually means-tested, that provide a form of income maintenance or replacement when people suffer through unemployment. This form of security is doubly entrenched in the MGNREGA scheme thanks to the provision of unemployment allowance inside it. If an applicant is not provided employment within 15 days of receipt of his application or from the date on which the employment has been sought, he/she is entitled to a daily unemployment allowance. This is also to keep the promise of guarantee that is the hallmark of its vision. The CAG Audit found that unemployment allowance was not paid in 58 of the surveyed blocks across 17 states. One of the main reasons for non-provision of dated receipts is the legal requirement for payment of unemployment allowance as mandated by the Act, in case employment is not provided by the state within the prescribed period. Further, the fact that unemployment allowance is to be paid by state governments appears to act as a disincentive for them to provide dated receipts. This situation needs to be tackled adequately. What seems important to me is the need to dispel the misunderstanding in the larger discourse that these are unwarranted commitments made by the State to the people who are completely dependent on its support.

Timely Payment of Wages

There are reports from the field that suggest that wage payments are often less than the notified wage, primarily due to inaccurate Schedule of Rates (SoRs), and delays in payment occur due to inadequate staff and other institutional constraints. To overcome these challenges, the Government of India has mandated that payments be made through bank and post office accounts of the beneficiaries (with certain exceptions as approved by the Government of India in advance). As a result, over 10 crore post/bank office accounts have been opened and

80 per cent of the total wages are being paid through these.

Wage Payment Less than the Notified Wage

In some states, the average wage is lower than the MGNREGA notified wage. Different reasons for this are the following:

(a) Since the MGNREGA wages are mostly calculated according to piece-rate (quantity of work output in a day), in some states, due to non-revision of SoRs, the average wage per day is less than the notified wage.

(b) Irregular supervision at worksites results in low productivity, which in turn results in lower wages. The factors responsible for this include a high composition of elderly men and women workers and non-uniform division into groups

Inadequate Staff

The MGNREGA faces shortage of staff as staff members are often given part-time responsibility, which leads to late measurement of works, ultimately leading to late payment of wages. The lack of staff is a real bottleneck in MGNREGA implementation, with serious consequences, especially for its bottom-up, people-centered architecture. The shortage of staff has had a serious impact on key parameters like high-quality, people-centered planning and implementation of works, availability of employment on time, timely measurements of works that are completed or in progress and hence, timely payments. The problem of inadequate staff and delayed measurements and payment gets further exacerbated during peak seasons, when the demand for work is at its highest.

Irregular Flow of Funds

It must be remembered that schemes like the MGNREGA are not meant only to do social welfare. Their structure of creating employment and giving wage is also meant to privilege work over welfare and create a condition, primarily economic, where this reversal finally changes the behavior of the people. The financial funding structure also reverses the federal hierarchies of the state and decentralize spending and fund generation both. The funds are allocated to states and districts based on an initial demand, at the beginning of the FY, and subsequently based on expenditure. Each district/block/gram panchayat is supposed to have spent at least 60 per cent of the funds to request for the next installment. There can be several time lags in this cycle; for instance, delay in updating expenditure records, delay in placing demand for additional fund by the district and scrutiny of expenditure and release of funds by the Government of India.

There may be further delays for the funds to reach the gram panchayat or field. The CAG audit, conducted in 2006, found that fund delays and procedural issues were caused due to non submission of appropriate documentation by blocks while applying for a subsequent installment of funds.

Recognizing that certain delays may be caused due to the time lag between demands for funds from districts and release of funds from the centre, the Government of India instructed the states to set up state funds in FY 2009-10. These funds would allow for bulk transfer of funds from the central government to the state. Following this, the state governments can allocate funds to districts as per the demand and later re-allocate funds, in case of unutilized funds, within the district without involving the central government in the process.

Payment through Banks and Post Offices and Financial Inclusion

Though instructions have been given to pay wages through bank and post office savings accounts, which have been issued to ensure transparency in wage payments and prevent misappropriations, there remain the areas for concern. The Government of India mandated that all MGNREGA wage payments should be made through bank/post office accounts opened in the name of the individual worker. As a result, nearly 10 crore bank/post office accounts of rural people have been opened under the MGNREGA and around 80 per cent of its payments are made through this route. Some states in northeast India including Manipur, Mizoram and Integrated Action Plan districts, after consultation with the central government, are still making payments in cash due to logistic reasons, mainly due to poor coverage of bank and post office accounts and security reasons. Tamil Nadu is the only other state that continues to make its wage payments in cash.

The problems in this regard pertain to the following aspects:

(a) There is poor coverage or network of banks and post offices in some areas, and in some cases, there is much distance from the nearest bank/post office, making it inconvenient for the beneficiary to collect payment through it.

(b) Often there is non-streamlined record-keeping at banks/post offices, primarily due to a lack of staff given the large volume of MGNREGA beneficiaries and payments. Other problems include non-updation of passbooks.

(c) Workers are often illiterate and do not get to open or operate their own accounts. In a survey conducted in Allahabad and Ranchi, only 28 per cent of the sample workers had opened their accounts on their own. Filling deposit and withdrawal slips is also a problem for the illiterate beneficiaries.

(d) A major problem faced by branch post offices is that their cash and line limit is very low, so there is need to raise their cash and line limit so that they are not strapped for funds while making payments to the MGNREGA workers.

The Government of India is currently pilot testing innovative ways for wage payment, including use of biometrics, smart cards etc.

Leakages and Misappropriations in the Scheme

An important ill that eats into the MGNREGA implementation is its serious criticism on account of perceived misappropriations and leakages. While there is no denying the fact that in several cases these are true, states are making progress by introducing payments through banks and post offices, as well as improving other aspects through other innovative means.

Some of the main hurdles in this aspect are:

(a) Wage payments to beneficiaries are calculated on the basis of attendance and measurements listed on muster rolls (MRs), which are supposed to be available at worksites and updated every day. However, studies that have conducted an MR verification indicate several irregularities in the filling and maintenance of these MRs.

Non-availability of Muster Rolls at Worksites/ Kutcha Entries in Muster Rolls

Muster rolls are at times not found at work-sites, the main reason for their being absent is that they are filled only after the completion of work. This problem has been common in many states across India. They were also not made available for CAG audit in many states.

Regular updation of muster rolls is important to ensure both accuracy and transparency in recording attendance. They are not updated as they ought to be. In the study they were found updated at 60 per cent of the worksites in Hoshiarpur district in Punjab and only at one worksite in Sirmaur district in Himachal Pradesh. Another study revealed similar findings in five districts of Uttar Pradesh. Their absence has also been reported by beneficiaries. Most of the worksites which do not keep proper muster rolls make non-permanent or kutcha entries for attendance, which can be exploited at ease.

Fake Entries in Muster Rolls

Yet another problem faced in muster rolls is that all entries are not genuine, chiefly aimed at exploiting the state funds, and resulting into leakages. A survey, conducted across different states in India, found leakages ranging from 5 to 33 percent. In some cases there were significant irregularities such as adjustments to the muster rolls. In addition, while there are instances of leakage on the ground, several states have taken initiatives to improve their monitoring and wage payment systems. To ensure that wage payment is made on time and transparently, states are trying different IT pilots. For example, in Sriganga nagar district, Rajasthan, a pilot on smart cards was tried in 2009 where one business correspondent (BC) was able to transact 1,400 daily wagers. This pilot was up-scaled, so that 25 of these correspondents were hired who could now serve 20,000 beneficiaries.

The incentive for the BC lies in the one-time fee of Rs. 4.50 for every smart card issued, which the bank bears. The bank also pays the correspondent a monthly stipend plus a small amount for every transaction.

While the smart card device is available on a rent of Rs. 9,000 each year, each smart card costs Rs. 112. The bank bears these costs. RBI reimburses Rs. 50 per smart card to the bank. Under the pilot, the bank has issued smart cards to the MGNREGA beneficiaries in 13 of the 20 branches they have in the district.

The advantages are obvious. The bank's reach has expanded because of the BCs, and time is saved in carrying out the transactions.

Similarly in Cuddalore district, Tamil Nadu, the women of Periyakanganankuppam village use the Automated Teller Machine (ATM). Fifteen months after the district started paying the MGNREGA wages through debit-card-linked-zero-balance accounts, the women have mastered the art of withdrawing their wages from the ATMs. These are different from the cash dispensers found in cities: in biometric ATMs the second level of authentication is one's fingerprint, not the personal identification number. The authentication leaves no scope for fraud because no one except the beneficiary can withdraw money. For the elderly and the unlettered, there is help available. In this village, Sudha, a resident with a school-leaving certificate to her credit, manages the ATM and helps people withdraw their earnings. The panchayat has also employed a resident who collects weekly workers' lists and their due wages from the worksite, and deposits cash with the bank. The bank, SBI, sends its staff to the village to put in cash in the machines. During the pilot, the Cuddalore block administration paid ₹ 12.25 lakh through 675 bank accounts in these two panchayats. ₹ 6.05 lakh was paid as cash to non-account holders. The Rural Tele-Banking Initiative under IIT Madras provided the technology. Periyakanganankuppam, with 445 account holders, and Pathirikuppam, with 230 account holders, successfully completed the pilot in May 2011. The plan is to upscale the project to all 145 villages in the Cuddalore block.

With a successful pilot in Tamil Nadu, the SBI is experimenting with a different technology in Odisha. The GPRS-enabled mobile phones are being used to enrol beneficiaries, as well as to make payments in this state. A not-for-profit is the BC for Odisha's pilot project, which started in November 2009. Each smart card carries details of the beneficiary and a unique ID. Option for voice verification also exists.

A cheque, with a list of beneficiaries and amount due to each, is issued by the sarpanch to the nearest State Bank of India branch. The bank credits the amount to beneficiary accounts, which gets credited to account of the BC. The money is then transferred to the BC representative (Customer Service Provider) at the gram panchayat level, who withdraws the amount and makes payments. Cost, however, is a deterrent and is the reason the pilot project was restricted to only some panchayats.

In Tamil Nadu, an innovative system is being used whereby each labourer has to enter his/her signature or thumbprint in the muster roll everyday by way of marking attendance. This ensures that not only are the muster rolls available for public scrutiny at the worksite, but also that a large number of people see them. Further the signatures/thumbprints make fudging difficult. This system has been further strengthened by regular worksite inspections.

Use of Contractor and Machinery

In many cases the contractors have been used, while the MGNREGA specifically prohibits the use of contractors and machinery for work to ensure that the labour is not exploited and benefits and wage payments are provided directly to the workers. However, in many cases, contractors were employed to complete several tasks. Similarly, it was found that machinery was used to clear shrubs and earthwork excavation in ordinary soil.

The cost of machinery was up to 72 per cent of the total cost of work. It was in clear contravention of the Act.

Payments to Fictitious (Ghost) Workers

There are field reports suggesting that in some cases wage payments are made to workers who either have no job cards or those who did not actually undertake work at worksites. Double payments have also been noted. Suitable action is being taken in such cases, still cases abound.

Transparency and Accountability

Under the Act, a gram sabha has to conduct regular social audits of all the projects taken up within the gram panchayat. Thus, the MGNREGA has inbuilt transparency and accountability mechanisms in its design, namely, pro-active disclosure and social audits. However, evidence from the field indicates that the frequency of social audits and their quality is a major constraint in effective implementation of the scheme. Findings from various field studies suggest that social audit is seldom carried out seriously, marring its quality and outcome.

There are good practices, however, where states have taken innovative steps towards developing and institutionalising accountability tools into the governance system. One of the most interesting examples of these innovations can be found in the state of Andhra Pradesh where the government has initiated a systematic process of undertaking social audits for all MGNREGA works across the state. This state has set up an independent directorate for conducting social audits and has demarcated a set percentage of funds (from the total funds that the state receives from the Government of India to ensure flexibility and independence of this unit. The social audit process hinges on participation of youth volunteers, normally from worker households, who are trained to accept complaints and survey records as well as generate awareness about the audit. The volunteers also conduct a cross-check of official records through a door to door verification of muster rolls and physical verification of works. On a pre-notified date, the reports, along with the findings of the social audit, are readout in public meetings attended by the labourers, official functionaries, political representatives and the media. The officials respond to the issues which are read out in public and take corrective action. Thus, it has helped to curb malpractices in this regard.

Interestingly, the Government of India, learning from the experience of Andhra Pradesh, has notified social audit rules, outlining in detail the processes and procedures for conducting quality audits by the state governments. Regular monitoring is done and regular follow-up with states is also undertaken.

Grievance Redressal

A tool for effective implementation of the Act remains grievance redressal system, which remains a cause for concern. Studies point out that it is necessary to strengthen grievance redressal systems to address issues of corruption as well as other process issues. While the Act provides for each state to formulate grievance redressal rules, few state governments have done so. In view of the need to strengthen grievance redressal, the Government of India has amended the MGNREGA Schedule to prescribe rules for speedy and effective disposal of complaints. The states have also been advised to set up district-level ombudsman to receive complaints from the MGNREGA workers and other stakeholders and facilitate their redressal. This has led to significant impact on generating awareness among beneficiaries as well as in improving quality of implementation of the scheme, as well as improved record of social audit. A study found that entries in job cards have increased from 39 per cent to 99 per cent following this step. It has also resulted into better facilities at worksites.

Management Information System (MIS) and Monthly Progress Report (MPR): An Overview

In 2006–07, the physical and financial performance of MGNREGA was monitored through MPRs, which were mostly hard copies of progress reports passed from the gram panchayats to the block to the district to be entered online. These reports could not be drilled down beyond the level of the district which made it difficult to monitor performance, issues and expenditure at the gram panchayat level. The MIS of the Government of India was developed to ensure intensive and real time monitoring, right up to the level of the gram panchayat. It is arguably the largest online database for a public programme. At present, there are 12 crore job cards, 100 per cent of them being on record, and 9 crore muster rolls uploaded on the MIS.

The MIS contains all relevant information about the beneficiary (including name, photograph, house location etc.), works (attendance of beneficiaries, location of work, person-days generated etc.), expenditure (amount spent on material, amount spent per work etc.) and other processes and procedures (delays in registration, wage payment etc.) There has been an increased thrust by the government to ensure that the state governments move from physical MPRs to real-time MIS. For FY 2011-12, more than 90 per cent of the total expenditure (as compared to MPRs) is available on the MIS. All MIS information is in public domain and is available at the level of the individual beneficiary. In other words, this information can be downloaded and cross verified in terms of work undertaken, payments made etc.

The MIS was created with a view to making the entire system under the MGNREGA foolproof, as can be seen from the above provisions, as one of the many concerns expressed about the scheme was that the administrative data may not be reflective of employment provided on the field. While this may be true to some extent, the MGNREGA is increasingly available online for cross verification. In FY 2011-12, more than 90 per cent of the total expenditure is available on MIS including details of beneficiaries etc. However, there is no denying that national-level studies would help resolve some of the discrepancies that have been brought to light. It may be noted the data on the MIS/MPR is real time.

There are reasons to believe that the programme can work towards the ends for which it was designed if a whole hearted attempt is made to work on it.

Conclusion

The MGNREGA has risen from strength to strength in all these years of its implementation, in which effort has been made to plug up its holes. It would be prudent to discuss some of the recent initiatives and reforms taken up by the Government of India as part of the next level of its implementation. Some of the steps can be discussed as hereunder.

List of Permissible Works Expanded

The list of permissible works under the MGNREGA has been expanded with a view to strengthen the positive synergy between MGNREGA and agriculture and allied rural livelihoods; to respond to the demands of the states for greater location-specific flexibility in permissible works; and to help improve ecological balance in rural India. Some of these works are new but many of them come within the category of works already permitted under the MGNREGA. The list responds to the demands from states for a more elaborate, specific and unambiguous list of works that could be taken up under the categories currently permissible.

While allowing to expand the list of works under the MGNREGA, the following conditions have to be followed:

(a) Only those works can be taken up that result in creation of durable assets.

(b) The order of priority of works will be determined by the gram panchayats concerned.

(c) 60:40 ratio for labour and material costs should be maintained at the gram panchayat level.

(d) No contractors/labour-displacing machinery can be used.

List of Works Allowed under the MGNREGA (Expanded)

Here is the list of works allowed under the MGNREGA as expanded now:

Fisheries-related works

- Fisheries in seasonal water bodies on public land

Works in coastal areas

- Fish drying yards
- Belt vegetation
- Construction of storm water drains for coastal protection

Rural drinking water-related works

- Soak pits
- Recharge pits

Rural sanitation-related works

- Individual household latrines
- School toilet units

- Anganwadi toilets
- Solid and liquid waste management

Flood management-related works

- Deepening and repair of flood channels
- Chaur renovation

Irrigation command-related works

- Rehabilitation of minors, sub-minors and field channels

Watershed-related works

- Contour trenches
- Contour bunds
- Boulder checks
- Farm bunding
- Gabion structures
- Underground dykes
- Earthen dams
- Dugout farm ponds
- Stop dams

Watershed-related works in mountain regions

- Spring-shed development

Agriculture-related works

- NADEP composting
- Vermi-composting
- Liquid bio-manures

Livestock-related works

- Poultry shelter
- Goat shelter
- Construction of cemented floor urine tank and fodder trough for cattle
- Azolla as cattle-feed supplement

Recording Demands under the MGNREGA

A major lacuna in implementation of the MGNREGA has been that states have not set up effective systems of recording demand. However, the new MGNREGA Guidelines enlist provisions for the states to overcome this. Some of these can be listed as follows:

(a) The provision for submitting applications for work must be kept available on a continuous basis through multiple channels so designated by gram panchayats, which may empower ward members, anganwadi workers, school teachers, self-help groups, village-level revenue functionaries, common service centres and MGNREGA labour groups to receive applications for work.

(b) Provision must also be made, wherever feasible, for workers to register applications for work through mobile phones in addition to the MGNREGA website and this should feed directly into the Management Information System (MIS).

(c) The gram panchayat or programme officer, as the case may be, shall be bound to accept valid applications and to issue a dated receipt to the applicant.

(d) Refusal to accept applications and provide dated receipts will be treated as a contravention under Section 25 of the MGNREGA.

(e) State governments have to ensure that the MIS will record the demand for work. Its monitoring system has to ensure that it captures even households that may have been purposely denied employment.

(f) To estimate demand in advance, the district administration may conduct a door-to-door survey of job card holders.

(g) The MGNREGA software will automatically generate the pay-order for payment of unemployment allowance to such wage seekers whose demand for work is not met within 15 days of demand. Reports prepared on this will have to be part of the essential set of reports to be tracked at the state level.

Effective Planning

Effective planning is the key to success so far as implementation of the MGNREGA is concerned. To adequately match the demand for work, prior assessment of the demand for work as well as its timing is required to be ascertained. Therefore, a list of works should be prepared in advance to meet this demand. This matching of demand and supply of work is the process of planning under the MGNREGA and is summed up as a labour budget for submission to the Government of India for fund allocation at the beginning of each financial year. Thus, a labour budget should reflect:

(a) Anticipated quantum of demand for work,

(b) Precise timing of the demand for work, and

(c) A plan that outlines the quantum and schedule of work to be provided to those who demand work.

This method can help to synchronise with the pattern of migration in an area so as to pre-empt distress migration. It must also be incumbent upon work-providers to pro-actively inform work-demanders well in advance about the schedule of work.

Strict Abidance by the Time Schedule

Under the current time schedule, annual plans have to be prepared outlining works to be undertaken in a gram panchayat as per the demand. They have to be presented for approval at the gram sabha around 2nd of October each year. However, this may be too late to prevent distress migration. In the absence of a timely work guarantee, households are likely to migrate after the kharif harvest season. It is, therefore, important for the gram panchayats to inform potential workers about availability of employment and timing of this employment well in advance of the kharif harvest. The Guidelines to the MGNREGA provide a time schedule to ensure that labour budgets are submitted in time by the states for approval by the Government of India, and allowing it time to communicate back to the concerned states and districts, so that the work can be begun in March and April each year.

Deployment of Additional Human Resources

It has been seen that there is need to deploy additional staff to aid with effective planning at the gram panchayat level, supervising the works and their monitoring of execution. The new guidelines point out the following:

- Each Block must appoint a full-time programme officer (PO) for the MGNREGA. For this purpose, the Block Development Officers (BDOs) or other block officers should not be given additional charge for the programme, as substitute for deploying a PO.
- Blocks will appoint at least three cluster-facilitation teams (CFTs) where either Scheduled Castes (SCs) or Scheduled Tribes (STs) or both form more than 30 per cent of the population or the annual MGNREGA expenditure exceeds ₹ 12 crore. Each of these three CFTs will service a cluster of gram panchayats, covering around 15,000 job cards or an area of about 15,000 hectares (ha). The CFT will comprise a fully dedicated, three-member professional, support team led by an assistant PO and include specialists in earthen engineering, community mobilisation, hydro-geology, and agriculture/allied livelihoods. This will also enable more professional planning based

on the watershed approach aimed at improved land and water productivity.

Reducing Delays in Wage Payments

The MGNREGA also guides in this respect. It specifies a payment schedule for states to follow and track, using a transactions-based MIS. It also suggests that the timeline for each process be determined and delays be monitored at each step through the MIS like closure of muster rolls (MR), capturing measurements, generating pay-order, issuance of cheques and pay-order to paying agency, transfer of cash to sub-agency (branch post office/business correspondent) and wage disbursement to workers.

Strengthening the MIS

The MIS is criticized for its inability to capture transactions on real-time basis and all data entries are basically post facto; for example, payments are entered in it after wages have been disbursed to workers. It is also criticized for delays in data reporting through the MIS. Therefore, the MGNREGA has worked out a strategy to address some of these issues by deploying a real-time transaction-based e-Governance solution in pilot districts. The first phase of the pilot will strengthen the electronic fund management system (e-FMS) leveraging the core banking system (CBS) of commercial banks. Subsequently this will also cover payments made through post offices and cooperative banks. In the second phase, field-level electronic data will be captured through handheld devices, which will also be used for demand registration, attendance, recording work measurements, etc.

(a) The Aadhaar is a unique identification number linked to a person's demographic and biometric information, which he can use to identify himself anywhere in India. It also serves as a basis to access a host of benefits and services. The Aadhaar number along with the job card number will now be part of the MIS to help eliminate non-genuine and duplicate job cards.

(b) Learning from the experience of states, the Government of India seeks to upscale the Business Correspondent (BC) model and is supporting its implementation. It has allowed ₹ 80 per account per year as incentive for the banks.

(c) Another major point of delay has been crediting of workers' bank accounts as this involves physical movement of cheques and wage lists from the gram panchayat to the bank after which banks are required to feed in details of the bank accounts of wage earners once again. To make this transaction seamless, the Ministry of Rural Development has worked with five banks in four states (Odisha, Gujarat, Rajasthan and Karnataka) to successfully develop electronic transfer of data files to banks. This solution is now being taken up in other states, as the system was found effective. A similar solution is being developed for transmitting data to head post offices which will cut down the time required for documents to travel.

Social Audit

To effectively implement social audit and be vigilant for transparency and accountability, the Government of India has notified, under the MGNREGA, social audit rules that mandate the establishment of a Social Audit Unit (SAU), to facilitate social audit by gram sabhas. An SAU can be either a society or a directorate, in each case independent of the implementing departments/ agencies. It will be responsible for building capacities of gram sabhas for conducting social audit by identifying, training and deploying suitable resource persons at village, block, district and state levels (drawing from primary stakeholders and other CSOs). It will create awareness amongst the labourers about their rights and entitlements under the Act and facilitate verification of records with primary stakeholders and worksites.

Performance Audit

To ensure further transparency and accountability, the social audit will be done by the Comptroller and Auditor General (CAG). All expenditure on the MGNREGA works will be audited both at the level of the central as well as state governments. In addition to the financial audit, the CAG will also conduct a performance audit with regard to these schemes. To begin with, such audits will be taken up in 12 states, and will be extended to the other with time.

Vigilance Cell

The Government of India has asked the states to set up three-tier vigilance mechanisms to pro-actively detect irregularities in the implementation of the Act as well as to follow up detected irregularities and malfeasance, including those identified during the social audit. At the state level, there will be a vigilance cell, headed by a chief vigilance officer, for this purpose.

Strengthening Section 25 of the Act

The guidelines emphasise that the states ensure careful implementation of the provisions of the Act. The following will be considered offences punishable under Section 25 of the Act:

(a) Job cards being found in the possession of any panchayat or MGNREGA functionary without plausible justification.

(b) Missing entries or delay in entries in the job card.
(c) Refusal to accept applications and provide dated receipts.
(d) Unreasonable delays in payment of wages.
(e) Failure to dispose of complaints within the stipulated time.

Limitations on Administrative Expenses

The MGNREGA provides 6 per cent of the total expenditure in a state as administrative expenditure. To ensure its strict compliance, the guidelines provide that at least two-thirds of this amount should be spent at the block-level and below. It has also been barred to acquire the following items under this head: new vehicles, new buildings, air-conditioners, and payment of salaries/remuneration/honoraria of functionaries who are not exclusively or wholly dedicated to the MGNREGA work.

While implementation remains uneven and patchy across states and districts, there is evidence to suggest that the MGNREGA has contributed to (a) increased rural wages everywhere; (b) reduced distress migration from traditionally migration-intensive areas; (c) usage of barren areas for cultivation; and (d) empowerment of the weaker sections and giving them a new sense of identity and bargaining power.

Though the achievements of the MGNREGA have been impressive, there have been issues with regard to its implementation that need to be recognized and addressed meaningfully. In the words of a passionate and optimistic scholar:

the isolation in which the nrega now operates must end—as a mere scheme of one ministry, and no more. This in fact is a programme of national importance which has been marginalised. While the ministry of rural development is the nodal ministry at the centre...the machinery of the entire government must act in concert, and conscious and systematic efforts made to marshal its combined energy, expertise and resource-as has been done only once before, for the green revolution.[29]

We must remember that MGNREGA does welfare work but it is not synonymous with welfare. It seeks to achieve much more than mere welfare which could have been done in many other ways, say through fiscal welfare or occupational welfare. The objectives of the scheme are much bigger and far reaching. In addition to relieving poverty, providing income maintenance and meeting special development needs of the society the scheme is also directed at streamlining other policy objectives and enhancing the living status of other rights in the society. The right to equality of sexes, of equitable income and fair opportunity, and to dignity of life are some that may be mentioned. It seeks to redistribute the primary and social goods in the society at both horizontal and vertical levels. For the nation to become truly independent and free, the MNREG Act has to be successful in the most substantial and creative measures that we discussed so far. And it can only happen if we understand its living career with sensitivity and dedication to the principles of our Constitution. This little book is dedicated to the hopes embodied in the Act and the dreams that sparkle in the eyes of those whom the Act touches.

□

Appendix – A
The Assertions Tested During the Survey of Hazaribagh District

(For detailed reference see Chapter 3)

Statements designed to evaluate the socio-cultural modernity of rural women:

1. All people should be equal.
2. Everyone is equal before the law.
3. In this democratic age, everyone should be respected.
4. One needs hereditary qualities to learn.
5. In all societies, there have always been high and low, and rich and poor persons. This will continue forever.
6. Women should not get high governmental job.
7. A wife should give better food to her husband than she takes herself.
8. Women cannot compete with men.
9. Men are more intelligent that women
10. Women should be paid less than men.
11. Children of upper castes should not play with children of lower castes.
12. The lower castes, as compared to upper castes, commit more crimes.
13. The lower castes, compared to upper castes, are less honest.

14. Persons of low castes do not learn the proper manner even if they get education and wealth.
15. One should get the blood of one's own caste, and not the blood of other caste.
16. A wife should have as much a right to remarry after the death of her husband as the man has after the death of his wife.
17. Ordinarily because the daughter does not get her share in the parental property, therefore, it is only proper that she gets a dowry.
18. It is in the interest of the women that they observe Purdah (veil system or seclusion) to protect themselves from the evil eyes of the society.
19. On the birth of a male child or on the sixth day of the birth, the friends and relations should be lavishly fed because the birth of a male child is an occasion for celebration.
20. The Shraddha or the last rituals of parents should be done properly even if one has to take a loan, because this offers peace to the soul of the deceased.
21. A man who does not believe in God and religion can never be a good person.
22. Though all religions preach love and brotherhood, yet it is true that violence and bloodshed have occurred due to religion.
23. It is not possible to have the same feelings of love towards people of other religions, as one has towards people of one's own religion.
24. The government should encourage marriages between people of different religions.
25. Only people of one's own religion help during one's bad days.

Inferences Drawn from the Responses

- The MGNREGA promotes equality, an important attribute of modernity.

- The MGNREGA promotes spirit of equality and flexibility.
- The MGNREGA workers certainly have more openness towards others' religion than those non-MGNREGA workers.
- The MGNREGA certainly promotes sense of openness.
- The MGNREGA instills sense of socio-cultural modernity among the respondents.

The computed value of statistic for socio-cultural modernity for experimental and control group is 5.78 which is larger than 1.645, this clearly indicates that the MGNREGA has impacted the socio-cultural modernity of rural women in a considerable way in favour of the Experimental Group.

Statements Designed to Evaluate Modernity of Attitude Towards Health

1. Life and death depends on God, medical treatment cannot do anything.
2. Good or bad health depends on the constitution of the baby. If the constitution of the person is good, he will keep good health even if he does not care for it.
3. Cancer is a contagious disease.
4. For a person to remain healthy, physical exercise and labour is necessary, whether one is a woman or a man.
5. During illness, a patient should either fast or should have light meal, because the patient has no power to digest.
6. Insanity is caused by evil spirits.
7. Once someone becomes insane, he can never be a completely normal person.
8. Mental illness is also a disease; therefore it should also be treated like other diseases.

9. Persons who have been once insane should never be entrusted with a responsible job.
10. Insanity can be cured by Sadhu/Fakir and magic.
11. It is better to take vitamin injection than to take milk, egg, fruits and other things to get vitamin.
12. Smoking, cigarette/bidi reduce tension; therefore, they are good for health.
13. Starch of rice is more beneficial to health.
14. Vegetable should be diced into small pieces, so that they can be boiled/cooked properly.
15. Sprouted corn is better for health.
16. Having two or three children is proper but they should be born within three or four years of marriage so that they can be brought up together.
17. The possibility of a child to be a boy or girl depends completely on the father's semen; it does not have any connection with the mother.
18. Birth of children is a gift of god. Therefore, whatever numbers of children in a family are, their birth should not be controlled.
19. A son is necessary for continuation of the lineage. Therefore, even after the birth of several daughters, the birth of children should not be checked until a son is born.
20. After the birth of two children, even if both are girls, a woman should get a tubectomy done, so that she does not have any more children.
21. Only doctors can treat minor or major illness properly; therefore, giving information to the mother can prove dangerous instead of being beneficial.
22. Main cause of children's disease is dirty water, therefore, they should always be given boiled water to drink.
23. A child is a lump of flesh and bones at the time of its birth. The brain starts developing after its birth.

24. The structure of bodies of children since birth is such that some weigh more and some less, therefore, weight has no important relation with health.
25. A three-four years old child needs the same amount of food as a grown up person, but he should eat several times.
26. First yellow milk from the mother's breast after child birth is harmful for the newly born baby.
27. A mother should not breastfeed her child during illness as it may cause harm to the child.
28. It is better to feed children tinned powder milk from bottle than mother's milk because tinned powder milk gives more strength.
29. The figure and beauty of a mother's body is spoiled if she breastfeeds her child.
30. When the child cries, the mother should immediately breastfeed it.

Inferences Drawn from the Responses

- The MGNREGA, in fact, provides a platform where knowledge on health is shared. The respondents in the experimental group are more aware on health issues.
- The MGNREGA workers strongly agree with health modernity statement.
- The MGNREGA workers have more knowledge about health issues than non-MGNREGA workers.
- The MGNREGA instills sense of learning new things regarding health.

The computed value of statistics for health modernity for experimental and control group is 6.33 which is larger than 1.645, this clearly indicates that the MGNREGA has had significant impact upon the health modernity of rural women in favour of the Experimental Group.

Statements Designed to Evaluate Modernity of Attitude Towards Politics

1. Democracy is not successful because illiterate persons have got the right to vote. Therefore, voting right should be given only to the educated persons.
2. To run an administration or government, one needs certain hereditary qualities.
3. As everyone has got the right to vote, poor and low castes are getting respect in the society. This is harmful to the society.
4. Democracy is the best political system as it offers an opportunity to change the government without violence and bloodshed.
5. Society can progress when the country has only one party which can form government and there should not be any opposition party.
6. It is a great meanness to give up one's own religion and accept another.
7. No man can be happy by marrying a woman of another religion.
8. The customs of different religions, such as Hinduism, Sikhism, Islam and Christianity vary, but the ideals of all are similar.
9. If blood transfusion becomes necessary in illness, one should take precaution that the blood given belongs to a person belonging to one's own religion.
10. All religions should be respected, but I believe that my religion is better than other religions.
11. Every citizen should have full freedom to speak against the government.
12. On radio the leaders opposing the government should get the same amount of time as is given to the leaders of the government.
13. A person who votes against the ruling party should be barred from government service.

14. Except the secret news about the defence of the country, newspapers should have full freedom to publish all kinds of news.
15. Newspapers should have full freedom to publish news and articles against the government.
16. We can develop our country only by strengthening our own religion and caste.
17. A man should be concerned with his village or town. What is happening in the country or abroad is of little importance to him.
18. If one cannot fight for his own caste or religion, he cannot fight for his own country.
19. An ordinary man should not involve himself in patriotism or service of the country. He should care for the welfare of his family.
20. Family is more important for a person than his country because it is the family which shares his joys and sorrows.
21. One should complain to the authorities if there are problems and difficulties in the society. One should not remain silent.
22. The politics these days is controlled by only gangsters; therefore, it is a waste of time to vote.
23. One should not concern himself with anything other than his job and family. Therefore, it is unnecessary to take interest in politics.
24. One will waste his entire life in fighting against dishonesty and injustice. Practical wisdom demands that one should get his work done by flattery, recommendation or even bribe.
25. It is enough that one builds up one's own life. He should not involve himself in improving the conditions of others.
26. A woman should not work if her husband earns enough to support his family.
27. Social and religious customs which are becoming

costly and causing economic strain should be discarded even if they are old and sacred.

28. It is difficult to succeed in this society; therefore, high aspirations lead to disappointment.
29. It is a good custom that offices are closed on death of someone because a dead person should be respected. Work, after all, is done sooner or later.
30. God has not created man. Man has slowly evolved from animals over millions of years.
31. Some persons are always engaged in work. They succeed in their work but they cannot enjoy life. I do not want such a life for me.
32. Any student can get a first class in examination if he works hard.
33. The main reason for the difficulties and worries of a person is his own mistakes and not his fate.

Inferences Drawn from the Responses

- The MGNREGA provides a platform for political education to rural women.
- It brings in a sense of equality.
- It strengthens the democratic process.
- It encourages openness towards religion.

The computed value of statistics for political modernity for experimental and control group is 5.4 which is larger than 1.645, this clearly indicates that the MGNREGA has impacted the political modernity of rural women in a considerable way in favour of the Experimental Group.

□

Reference

Afridi F. et al, 'Female Labour Force Participation and Child education in India: The Effect of the National Guarantee Scheme', Discussion Paper 6593, Institute for the Study of Labour, Bonn, 2012.

Agarwal Bina, A Field of One's Own: Gender and Land Rights in South Asia (Cambridge: Cambridge University Press, 1996) p. 9.

Beteille, Andre. 'Constitutional Morality', Economic and Political Weekly, Vol. 43, No. 40 (Oct. 4-10, 2008), pp. 35-42, p. 35.

Bhatt, Wasudha. 'The Gender Dimension of Migration in India: The Politics of Contemporary Space in Orissa and Rajasthan' in Development in Practice, Vol. 19, No. 1 (Feb., 2009), pp. 87-93.

Constituent Assembly Debates, (New Delhi: Lok Sabha Secretariat, 1961).

Dreze, Jean & R. Khera, 'The Battle for Employment Guarantee' in Frontline, 3 January 2011.

J. Ghosh, 'Migration and public policy', Frontline 22 (10): 2005

Hirway, Indira. 'Providing Employment Guarantee in India: Some Critical Issues' in Economic and Political Weekly, Vol. 39, No. 48 (Nov. 27-Dec. 3, 2004), pp. 5117-5124.

Khera, Reetika ed., The Battle for Employment Guarantee (New Delhi: Oxford University Press, 2011).

Khera, Reetika and Nandini Nayak, 'Women Workers and Perceptions of the National Rural Employment Guarantee Act,' Economic and Political Weekly, Vol. 44, No. 43 (October 24-30, 2009), pp. 49-57.

Mathur, Lalit. Employment Guarantee: Progress so Far,

Economic and Political Weekly, Vol. 42, No. 52 (Dec. 29, 2007-Jan. 4, 2008), pp. 17-20.

Narayananan, Sudha. 'Employment Guarantee, Women's Work and Child Care, in Economic and Political Weekly, March 1, 2008.

National Federation of Women, 'Socio-economic Empowerment of women under NREGA, Report to the Ministry of Rural Development, 2008.

Nguyen, Liem, Brenda S. A. Yeoh, and Mika Toyota, 'Migration and the well-being of the "left behind" in Asia', Asian Population Studies 2 (1): 2006.

Papanek, Hannah. Family Status Production: The "Work" and "Non-Work" of Women, Signs, Vol. 4, No. 4, The Labor of Women: Work and Family (Summer, 1979), pp. 775-781.

Patnaik, Prabhat. 'On the Need for Providing Employment Guarantee' in Economic and Political Weekly, Vol. 40, No. 3 (Jan. 15-21, 2005), pp. 203-207.

Rawls, John. A Theory of Justice (Cambridge, MA: The Belknap Press of the Harvard University Press, 1971; rev. edn. 1999).

Sen, Amartya and Jean Dreze, An Uncertain Glory: India and Its Contradictions (London: Allen Lane, 2013).

Sen, Amartya. Development as Freedom (New Delhi: Oxford University Press, 2000).

Stone, P. A. Development and Planning Economy: Environmental and Resource Issues (London and New York: E. & F. N. SPON, 2005).

http:// www.unhcr.ch/development/governance-01.html

□

Endnotes

1. *The Constitution of India*, Article 39.
2. John Rawls, *A Theory of Justice* (Cambridge, MA: The Belknap Press of the Harvard University Press, 1971; rev. edn. 1999) p. 53. Emphasis added.
3. Rawls, Ibid., p 72.
4. Amartya Sen and Jean Dreze, *An Uncertain Glory: India and Its Contradictions*(London: Allen Lane, 2013) p. 273.
5. Sen and Dreze, Ibid., p. 275.
6. Indira Hirway, 'Providing Employment Guarantee in India: Some Critical Issues' in *Economic and Political Weekly*, Vol. 39, No. 48 (Nov. 27-Dec. 3, 2004), pp. 5117-5124, p. 5117.
7. Indira Hirway, 'Providing Employment Guarantee in India: Some Critical Issues' in *Economic and Political Weekly*, Vol. 39, No. 48 (Nov. 27-Dec. 3, 2004), pp. 5117-5124, p. 5117.
8. Amartya Sen and Jean Dreze, *An Uncertain Glory: India and Its Contradictions* (London: Allen Lane, 2013) p. 202.
9. Jean Dreze and R Khera, 'The Battle for Employment Guarantee' in Frontline, 3 January 2011; Also see Reetika Khera ed. *The Battle for Employment Guarantee* (New Delhi: Oxford University Press, 2011)
10. Prabhat Patnaik, 'On the Need for Providing Employment Guarantee' in *Economic and Political Weekly*, Vol. 40, No. 3 (Jan. 15-21, 2005), pp. 203-207, p. 203.
11. See National Federation of Women, 'Socio-economic Empowerment of women under NREGA, Report to the Ministry of Rural Development, 2008; Sudha Narayananan, 'Employment Guarantee, Women's Work

and Child Care, in *Economic and Political Weekly*, March 1, 2008; F Afridi et al, 'Female Labour Force Participation and Child education in India: The Effect of the National Guarantee Scheme', Discussion Paper 6593, Institute for the Study of Labour, Bonn, 2012; among others.

12. Hannah Papanek, Family Status Production: The "Work" and "Non-Work" of Women, *Signs*, Vol. 4, No. 4, The Labor of Women: Work and Family (Summer, 1979), pp. 775-781, p. 780.
13. Hannah Papanek, Family Status Production: The "Work" and "Non-Work" of Women, *Signs*, Vol. 4, No. 4, The Labor of Women: Work and Family (Summer, 1979), pp. 775-781, p. 780.
14. Reetika Khera and Nandini Nayak, 'Women Workers and Perceptions of the National Rural Employment Guarantee Act,' *Economic and Political Weekly*, Vol. 44, No. 43 (October 24-30, 2009), pp. 49-57, p. 56.
15. Ibid.
16. B.R. Ambedkar, *Constituent Assembly Debates*, 4th November, 1948.
17. Andre Beteille, 'Constitutional Morality' *Economic and Political Weekly*, Vol. 43, No. 40 (Oct. 4-10, 2008), pp. 35-42, p. 35.
18. During the research, some very interesting questions were asked to bring out the responses from the respondents so that we could deduce our inferences. Some of the pertinent assertions on which their responses were sought and the above inferences were drawn are added as **Appendix A** of the book.
19. Amartya Sen, Development as Freedom (New Delhi: Oxford University Press, 2000) p. 189.
20. J. Ghosh, 'Migration and public policy', Frontline 22 (10): 2005, p. 20.
21. Liem Nguyen, Brenda S. A. Yeoh, and Mika Toyota, 'Migration and the well-being of the "left behind" in Asia', *Asian Population Studies* 2(1): 2006, 37-44.
22. Wasudha Bhatt, 'The Gender Dimension of Migration in India: The Politics of Contemporary Space in Orissa and Rajasthan' in *Development in Practice*, Vol. 19, No. 1 (Feb., 2009), pp. 87-93, 93.

23. P.A.Stone, *Development and Planning Economy: Environmental and Resource Issues* (London and New York: E. & F. N. SPON, 2005) p. 1.
24. Patnaik, ibid.
25. Dreze and Sen, op cit., p. 205.
26. Ibid.
27. Bina Agarwal, *A Field of One's Own: Gender and Land Rights in South Asia* (Cambridge: Cambridge University Press, 1996) p. 9.
28. http:// www.unhcr.ch/development/governance-01.html
29. Lalit Mathur, Employment Guarantee: Progress so Far, *Economic and Political Weekly*, Vol. 42, No. 52 (Dec. 29, 2007-Jan. 4, 2008), pp. 17-20, p. 20.